THE WAR

A COLLECTION OF REAL LIFE STORIES TO
EMPOWER THE WOMEN TO FACE THE
CHALLENGES, TO BE RESILIENT IN TOUGH
SITUATIONS AND TO EMERGE AS WARRIORS

DR. VIJAYALAKSHMI ALURI

Copyright © Dr. Vijayalakshmi Aluri
All Rights Reserved.

ISBN 978-1-63806-893-8

This book has been published with all efforts taken to make the material error-free after the consent of the author. However, the author and the publisher do not assume and hereby disclaim any liability to any party for any loss, damage, or disruption caused by errors or omissions, whether such errors or omissions result from negligence, accident, or any other cause.

While every effort has been made to avoid any mistake or omission, this publication is being sold on the condition and understanding that neither the author nor the publishers or printers would be liable in any manner to any person by reason of any mistake or omission in this publication or for any action taken or omitted to be taken or advice rendered or accepted on the basis of this work. For any defect in printing or binding the publishers will be liable only to replace the defective copy by another copy of this work then available.

To all the Women

Contents

Foreword — vii

Preface — xi

Acknowledgements — xiii

1. The War (against The Invisible) — 1
2. The Flower Garden — 16
3. Break The Shackles — 25
4. Quagmire — 39
5. The Path — 48
6. The Burning Furnace — 60
7. Fragrance — 70

About The Author — 85

Foreword

A sentence with intimacy

Stories that began in the vocal form of 'once upon a time' in the early days underwent many changes after being put into written form. It may not be related to the narrative mentioned in the Agnipurana, but to the narratives flowing in modern literature. Stories change from time to time in form and style.

However, whether it is the story of Chandamama or Chamballoyagatha, it should move the thoughts of the readers. Renowned literary critic, Mr Rachamallu Ramachandra Reddy said that stories should be born out of life... The truths of life should be shown in close-up and give the reader an understanding of life. We need to broaden the horizons of our readers. "

Filled with such excellent qualities and goals, Dr Aluri Vijayalakshmi's stories strike a balance between feeling and thought and knocking at the door of our hearts. Literature plays a major role in shaping ethnic culture.

Vijayalakshmi is invading social injustices by using storytelling as a weapon. The unrest and conflict that is raging internally and externally in a woman's life are literalized. The extraordinary personalities and absurdities that appear in the stories that some people write are nowhere to be seen in these stories.

Fragnance: Incidents such as frequent honour killings and gang rapes in recent times are scattering caltrops on the paths of women's lives. Though they didn't always make sensational news in the media, there was a realistic representation of different issues that are longitudinally splitting the lives of women. Moving away from the husband who became a slave of addictions and abusing his wife dreadfully and the parents and brothers, who were under self-deception with the burden of tradition, how a woman faces challenges and hurdles at every step in the migrated place in the process of constructing a new life, make the reader excited.

Break the Shackles: The author says that many husbands may have different mentalities, but their mentality and behaviour is almost the same with a minor difference in the case of the wife. The story brandishes the whip on the arrogant husbands who might appear modern physically, but mentally feel that the wife is a slave to the husband.

Some new generation feminists are bypassing the real issues of women and are indulging in unnecessary controversies. In such an environment, the 'Break the shackles' story appears as a lamp lit in the pitch darkness.

The story tells loudly that the oppressed woman needs justice; mere help is not enough – The story 'break the shackles inspires and provokes the women to assert and emancipate from the shackles of Patriarchal model of family and society

Burning Furnace: The story represents the anger of the affected people on the anti-people policies of the Government, that is acquiring thousands of acres of land in the name of the special economic zone. It blatantly criticizes the disgraceful attitude of the Governments, that are supposed to protect the common people, acting as middlemen and acquiring the land by threatening the people and forcing them to surrender and leave form their land, sometimes from their village and often from their lives.

The story questions the sanctity and need of the model of development that would destroy the lives of many people and frankly declares that this development is not for the benefit of common people, but, for the development of a handful of rich and powerful.

The story illustrates how many families and lives are affected, not only directly but also indirectly, by the new economic policies and gives a hope that the constant anger of the affected people against Governments and corporate powers would be successful.

Flower garden: George Bernard Shaw once said that 'money alone is greater than money'. But the story 'Flower garden' tells that there are many joys and values which wouldn't be bought or measured by the money. The story also reveals that there is a wide gap between one's social status and culture, she or he nurtures.

In the rest of the stories, the author's voice is very sharp with discretion and highly intense while analysing the different social issues. But this story filled with sentimentality in every word haunts us with the tragic tone of the famous singer Saigals' song

Quagmire: 'Quagmire' is like X-ray, which shows how easily the drugs are available as chocolates to the youth in the colleges, universities and even in the schools, leading the youth into the dangerous paths and how their future is destroyed by the addictions.

The Path: This story rightly reflects the new addictions in modern society that are ruining the lives of youth and shows them a golden path to transform as socially productive citizens

The War: Many authors have forgotten that literature is heart-related. Huge bundle of Corona poetry without any humane touch had been published in the recent turbulent months testing the reader's patience. While such artificial works were floating abundantly, 'The war' had emerged as a powerful story to infuse human values into the people who are struggling to cope up in the corona affected environment.

The author, who fondly cherishes and values the best culture in life and literature, has translated her own experiences into the story 'The war'.

Last but not the least, Dr Aluri Vijayalakshmi is undoubtedly one of the few writers after Mrs Ranganayakamma who write with social responsibility and clear understanding!

Adrusta Deepak
Renowned Progressive poet, Lyric writer of movies
& critic

Preface

These real life stories reflect women's grit to empower themselves challenging the discrimination, injustice, exploitation and different forms of violence oppressing them; the culture, social norms and Government policies that are devastating their lives and also how the lives of misguided youth are being destroyed in the present day socio-cultural and political environment.

Acknowledgements

I humbly acknowledge the valuable guidance, inspiration and positive push of Mr Som Bathla, without which publishing of this book might not be realty.

I am highly indebted to Mr Adrusta Deepak, a renowned progressive poet, lyric writer for many successful Telugu movies and an acclaimed critic of Telugu literature, for writing a crisp and genuine foreword.

I profusely thank Mrs Durga and Mrs Niraja Bandi who have edited the stories with lot of diligence and interest.

I also thank Mrs.Sudha Maganti and Dr. Bharathalakshmi for their help and motivation

I am also grateful to Mr Praneeth Chandra for his support in publishing the book

CHAPTER ONE

The War (against the invisible)

*Dedicated to all obstetricians and pregnant women in Corona Pandemic time

Uma woke up with the melodious and pleasant chirping of birds. Lazily, she got up from the bed and drew the window curtains aside. Of late, Mother Nature had regained a little of her original pristine beauty with pollution being on the wane. Nature appeared clean and fresh.

While the whole world is fighting with an invisible common enemy, every human being in this world is fighting varied types of wars, a war against fear, a war against insecurity, a war against hunger, a war against one's own soul etc.

Musing over this, Uma stretched herself to shake off the sleep and reached out to her cell and began accessing the WhatsApp 'Young mothers to be' group and started typing the replies to the queries posed by the group members.

She got busy typing suggestions about the lifestyle modifications, needed investigations, treatment and the answers for varied queries posted by pregnant women. While at the task, her mind dwelt on the unprecedented time the whole world was going through with the novel coronavirus posing a mortal threat to mankind.

Dr Uma was annoyed by the sudden and unexpected situation of having to give advice and treatment suggestions without testing the patients.

The lockdown, which was imposed throughout the nation, after experimenting with a day of the curfew that did not yield the expected results, had brought the lives of all and sundry to a grinding halt. Everyone accepted it as the best way to outsmart the vile virus but slowly the ramifications started hitting people.

Despite all the services, requiring an interface with the public had ceased, doctors, whose services were indispensable and as there is no alternative to their professional expertise had the 'front line warrior' epithet thrust upon them. The doctor community, rising to the occasion, started showing their concern, by way of reaching out to their patients through WhatsApp messages, audio and video calls.

Dr Uma was frustrated with the situation as she was unable to reach out to her patients in person but at the same time, she was grateful to the technology as she could at least reach out to them virtually and alleviate fears of her patients albeit in a small way.

The shrill ring of the phone jolted her back from her deep contemplations about the agonizing situation. On picking up the phone she heard the anxious tone of one of her patients.

"Hello! Madam! It's me Prashanthi", Have you seen the message I posted in the group?" she continued. "I have pain in my lower back and abdomen and I frequently have to visit the washroom. I could hardly sleep for the entire night. I am still a week away from entering the ninth month. Will I have premature delivery? I am worried Madam."

enquired Prashanthi as her voice quivered with pent up fear and anxiety.

Uma enquired other details of Prasanth's complaints and made some suggestions

"What am I to do if the pain doesn't abate? Shall I come to the Hospital? ... How can I reach the Hospital? No public vehicles are moving since Lockdown.... Do you think I could ride pillion on my husband's motorbike? I got to know from my friends that most of the hospitals are closed and even if they are open, only emergencies are attended to. Will you be coming to the hospital to attend to me Madam?" the anxious voice poured out all the misgivings.

"If you don't get relief by today evening, come to the hospital once. I will come and see you. Now follow my instructions and take proper rest and relax. Don't get tensed up." Uma tried to soothe Prasanthi's frayed nerves with her calm and tender tone.

"What else is there except tension Madam? I am afraid, if I come to the hospital, I might get Corona infection. If I don't come to the hospital and get tested by you, I am worried about my health and my unborn child's wellbeing. If you put your hand on my belly and tell me that both of us are alright, it assures me so much." Prasanthi's voice reflected her despair and anxiety

"I know we are going through the most trying times, fighting this unprecedented contagion. We have to accept and adjust to the present situation and act accordingly to save our lives.... O.K. don't worry." said Uma gently, trying to infuse confidence in the disturbed person.

"What if I contract the virus and what if it gets transmitted to the baby, just the thought is unbearable and making me extremely restless. I am going mad seeing the visuals on T.V., displaying the tragic incidents of some pregnant women dying as they are denied admission and timely care by the hospitals if there is a suspicion of the person having corona infection."Uma could gauge the agitation in Prashanthi from her terrified voice.

"Spend less time watching TV or better still just avoid TV viewing. No harm at all. Instead, spend the time listening to good soothing music and reading good books. As you are not moving out of your house, you may feel low and gloomy. Get connected with your near and dear ones, relatives and friends, by making a telephone call or messaging, enquire about their well-being, share with them the safety measures that you are following and discuss your experiences in this crucial period. That will promote a strong bond with them and reduce your anxiety. If you have a severe problem, come to the Hospital." Uma suggested with a cool voice.

"There is no clear evidence that an unborn child gets corona infection from its mother, as of now, there is almost no risk. Moreover, at the moment, what we know about the new Coronavirus is very minimum, daily there is new information and new guidelines are being released. Now, don't bother about all these things. Be relaxed" Uma's mind was quite disturbed even after she switched off her mobile.

Uma's thoughts wandered to the past. She was the first one to hold Prashanthi, as a baby, as she had delivered her. Since the time of Prasanthi's arrival, the ties between the two families got bolstered.

Prashanthi had not heeded either Uma's or her mom Devaki's advice of conceiving a baby at the proper time as she had her career as her top priority. When she finally came around to have a baby, she had to face complications.

When all her interventions, as an obstetrician, came to nought, she referred her to a fertility expert who was her acquaintance. IVF (In Vitro Fertilization)provided succour to Prashanthi and she finally got the much-awaited pregnancy. But since conception, Prashanthi had been facing one problem or the other during the first six months of her pregnancy causing much agony. Just when Prashanthi had come to manage the pregnancy well and got a bit stable after entering the seventh month, she was faced with the new challenge of the vicious novel coronavirus.

Uma had been trying her best in providing support and proper guidance to her pregnant patients with difficulties and alleviating their anxieties through messages.

But her worry was about the high-risk group of pregnant women and those in the last days of the third trimester and close to the delivery time.

'Without close monitoring and regular check-ups, how will these women tide over any sudden adverse situation and if it goes untreated what will be the plight of the mother and the baby?' These thoughts made Uma feel helpless.

Since the implementation of the lockdown, Uma had to don the caps of a maid as well as a cook. As she was about to enter the kitchen to make her morning cup of coffee, she got held up as the phone rang again. It was her friend and classmate Kavitha.

Uma's classmates and friends, who were too busy with the demands of one's own life, paused for a little while and have been trying to connect and bond with each other, trying to know about each other's wellbeing, called each other to know how each one was spending time during this difficult time.

Most of Uma's friends had retired barring a few like Kavitha, a gynaecologist. Uma and Kavitha being gynaecologists, have been attending to emergency cases.

They discussed the stress they were experiencing while working under the threat of Corona.

They felt happy for the humane services extended by doctors who worked in Covid centres and condemned some incidents of attacks on them. Both felt aggrieved as they recounted the passing away of a well-known senior doctor who had succumbed to corona while in the line of duty and thereby could not even get a respectable funeral. They cracked jokes about their old age aches and pains and had a hearty laugh.

"As medical students, we always felt that mosquitoes causing the then rampant malaria and filaria were true socialists as they affected everyone alike, without any discrimination of class, caste, colour etc. But now the novel coronavirus has proved to be a greater socialist, equally terrorizing the privileged and the common man alike" Kavitha commented with a laugh.

But both of them knew very well that, it was only half the truth. Both understood well the implicit veracity of those words. Uma's thoughts once again went to the lockdown travails and how it had brought to the fore, the gaping inequalities in the society.

The miserable plight of displaced, homeless and daily wagers who had migrated from villages to the cities long back in search of better incomes, now lost their livelihoods. They are returning to their villages, hundreds of miles away, on foot, along with their children, old parents and pregnant women. This presented a pathetic picture of human suffering.

The untold misery of the migrant workers cannot be compared to the rest of the well-heeled populace who stayed put in the cosy confines of their homes without any apprehensions about their upkeep.

Finally, they wound up the conversation after chatting about the difficulties being faced by everyone during the lockdown period.

Uma's cup of coffee had to be postponed once again as she was stopped from entering the kitchen with the phone ringing yet another time.

"Mom! what are you doing?" It was Radhika from Canada.

"Just done with sending messages to my patients," said Uma, knowing pretty well that her answer would irk her daughter to no end.

"Mom! Won't you listen to us? No amount of our pleading seems to deter you from going to the hospital." Radhika's voice was an amalgamation of anger and aggression. Uma was well aware that her daughter's anger was justifiable, as she was in the high-risk group for corona infection, as she had crossed seventy years and was a chronic asthma patient.

In a gentle voice trying to alleviate the fears of her daughter, Uma said, "I have stopped attending outpatients and I am going to the hospital only for emergencies. But...unless I respond and connect with my patients, who repose a lot of confidence in me, they feel agitated." Uma said trying to cajole her daughter.

Uma knew that Shashank, who worked in the same hospital as a neurologist, was apprising his elder sister about how she was attending to emergency cases, deliveries and Caesarians as well. Shashank requested his mother not to get exposed to the patients, to assign her work to a junior Gynecologist till the corona subsided and a semblance of normalcy was restored.

Shashank had already requested the hospital authorities to relieve her from her duties and post a youngster in her place. He might have informed all this to his sister.

Both Radhika and her brother were trying their level best to stop their mother from going to the hospital. Uma knew that her children were extremely worried about her safety.

"Mom!" continued Radhika, trying to convince her mother. "You have been toiling for the past fifty years without a day of rest. I still remember very vividly how you went back to work after a mere fifteen-day rest when Shashank was born after a C-section. Mom! I know that your profession is your life and soul. I also know that your work is your rest, your happiness, your health and your purpose of living.

But now the situation is quite different, appears extremely dangerous. God forbid, if something happens to you, what if you fall prey to the viral infection? It is going to be the most dreaded situation which, I am afraid, we can't bear.

Shashank has been telling me that it upsets him to see you rush, at unearthly hours, to the hospital to attend to emergencies. He is immensely pained that he is unable to convince you to temporarily stop your work. Every day he has been calling me and sharing his angst. Mom! Please try to understand." The last words were barely audible as Radhika's voice choked with emotion.

Uma understood that her son, who could see her rush to the hospital, from his flat right above hers, had been extremely distressed by her obstinate stance. The concern being shown by her children moved her to tears.

"No dear! I cannot refuse to see my patients who have been under my care all these days. If I escape from attending them at the end in these difficult times, I will not feel comfortable with myself.

I know the gravity of the situation. Whatever precautions I might take, if I go to the hospital, I am at high risk of getting the infection. If I am infected, I can imagine the plight of you both." Uma paused for a moment and gathered herself.

"For a while I ponder, the world will not stop if I don't attend to the patients. Many doctors in this city can take care of them; I am not the only one. As per your wish, I could stay back at home. But then my soul cries, 'Isn't my duty similar to that of a soldier in wartime! Doesn't he fight unto death? He will not run away, will he? I feel it is inhuman to run away to protect myself without attending to the patients" Uma's voice trembled.

"Mom! Maybe you are right. Whatever you told, might be true. I understand your feelings, but my concern is about you and your safety. For us you are precious. We do not want to lose you. Though it is already two years since Dad passed away, we are still unable to come to terms with the loss. Now we don't want to lose you too." Radhika choked over the phone, in turn breaking down Uma's strong resolve.

"Alright. I shall stop going to the hospital. Stop crying." said Uma, trying to pacify her daughter. A greatly relieved Radhika hung up the phone after further chatting with her mother about her kids and husband.

After having her breakfast, Uma answered the queries of her patients, attended their video and audio calls.

"Do I have to stop this messaging as well from tomorrow?" pondered Uma and a wry smile crossed her face.

Uma spent the rest of the day enjoying old Telugu songs rendered by Bhanumathi – a popular singer and actor of yore; from afternoon till nine in the night, her time was consumed with a series of Webinars of Obstetrics and Gynecology, which had become the order of the day with the corona effect. Again, she saw patients' messages and answered them.

As she was about to call it a day, remembering her promise to Radhika, Uma called the hospital receptionist and informed her to entrust the newly appointed young gynaecologist, Dr Swapnika, with emergency cases.

Having kept up her promise, Uma went to bed with a light heart only to be woken up with a call from the hospital around 1 A.M. She was informed about Divya, a patient in labour, and the inability of Dr Swapnika making it to the hospital as her young son was down with high temperature. Dr Swapnika called Uma and explained to her how her son was refusing to let her leave his bedside. Uma could understand the young mother's plight.

In the wake of the lockdown, Divya's schedule of regular checkups was hampered. She was brought to the hospital two days back with severe headache, giddiness and vomiting. Uma checked her, got the scan done and informed her attendants that she had high blood pressure, one of the twins died in the uterus and the gestational age of the live fetus corresponded to the beginning of the ninth month.

The news had a devastating effect on Divya. Uma placated the fears of the family members about the viability of the second fetus and the threat to the mother and promised them that she would handle the crucial situation safely. She had administered appropriate medicines to stabilize the patient's condition

She told the attendants that Divya needed to be given injections for two consecutive days for the safety of the live child and she would try to bring down the blood pressure meanwhile and deliver the child that morning by cesarean section. She advised them to admit Divya in the hospital immediately as she needed vigilant supervision. Uma instructed to get some blood and urine tests also done and reserve one unit of blood.

But as soon as Divya was a little bit better after medication, Divya's attendants wanted to take her home as that day was not auspicious, get the second dose of injection administered at home and admit her for delivery that morning, not heeding Uma's instructions that the patient needed the proficient supervision of the experienced hospital staff. Now Divya came in a situation of crisis.

Uma fell in a dilemma after she received the call from the hospital emergency, whether to go and attend to the patient at risk or not, as per the promise she made to her daughter. But the hesitation was momentary as she decided instantly to go and attend to Divya.

Divya's face brightened as soon as she saw Uma coming towards her

"I have been getting labour pains for one hour. I am unable to feel the baby's movements properly. The staff here told me that some other doctor will attend my case instead of you. My heart stopped beating for a minute and I am too worried. Madam! I am glad that you have come. Now that you are here, I am rest

Swinging into action, Uma scanned the fetus and found that there was no cause for alarm and relayed the same to Divya who sighed with relief

"My brother went to the blood bank to get the blood. My sister's blood also is AB negative. She donated one unit of blood yesterday, it matched with my blood. Blood bank people kept the blood ready to issue after doing the screening tests." Uma removed her gloves and began writing the notes of her findings and instructions.

Just then a pregnant woman was carried into the emergency ward. She was having fits, with her whole body shaking, eyeballs rolled up and her sari was drenched in blood. The attendants were crying loudly and pleading to save her life.

"She has been suffering from fever and cough for four days. Pains started about five hours back. While we were thinking of taking her to the hospital, she has got fits. Immediately we took her to a hospital. They refused to admit her with a suspicion of Corona infection.

We took her to four more hospitals, but everywhere, we got the same reply. She kept on getting fits and we panicked. We are afraid, She will die if she is not treated immediately. Please save her, Please!" The attendants were begging the staff. Uma who had just done with Divya's admission notes, got up to check the patient.

Casualty Staff, dressed like astronauts as a part of preventive measures, looked at Uma who was rushing towards the patient who might have had Corona infection, with bewilderment and scepticism.

"Madam! The patient has a high fever and cough. Her blood pressure is very high, and she is having heavy bleeding. She didn't have any checkups previously. We need to do a Covid test along with other investigations. Shall we admit her with so much risk involved or send her away?" The casualty medical officer who had elicited the history from the attendants asked Uma hesitantly.

'True. It is risky. If we don't treat her immediately, there is a sure risk of her death, if we are unable to save her, there is the risk of us being abused and beaten up, risk of hospital premises and equipment being destroyed, by the people who are begging to treat her now. All this is a possibility.

There will be a complete volte-face in the attitude of the attendants; they will conveniently forget their culpability of not seeking medical attention on time and resort to violence.

The ubiquitous electronic media rushes to the scene and the focus of the cameras will be on our faces, broadcasting this episode to the whole world repeatedly portraying the doctor as the arch-villain. But how tragic it is to lose a life because the right treatment is not given at the right time?' Uma pondered.

"Well, Doctor! I do agree that it is wise to weigh the risks involved in the case, but don't you agree being doctors it is our prime responsibility to save a life." With these words, Uma quickly got down to delegating duties to the nurses and the duty doctor.

"If we deliver the baby through caesarean, the convulsions can be controlled. Please inform the patient's attendants about the possible risks involved and take their signature on the consent form. I will also counsel them.

Get all the tests done including viral screening and Covid test. The Covid test result cannot be procured immediately. But it would help in post-operative management. We shall anyway adhere to universal precautions. Arrange for blood, the patient looks very pale. Inform the anaesthetist, paediatrician and OT personnel. Quick." Having instructed everyone around her she began to scan the patient to assess the status of the baby.

"Madam, Shashank sir gave us strict instructions that we shouldn't call you under any circumstance in the present situation. Divya being your patient we could not avoid calling you. If sir comes to know about this case, he will be furious. And God forbid, if you were to contract the virus, we can never be at peace with ourselves." The duty doctor vented his fear in a soft tone.

Uma tried her best to assuage his fears. But she knew the consequences of contracting the disease-the tests, quarantine, numerous medicines to take, fear, anxiety, loneliness, depression, ending up on a ventilator etc. is a dreadful prospect.

Also fresh in her mind was the incident of a practising doctor with a long-term experience, who had laid down his life after getting infected while in the line of duty.

Such morbid thoughts did not shake Uma's resolve since she felt that remaining insensitive and inert was inexcusable despite possessing the necessary skill and proficiency to save a life.

By the time the patient was prepared for the surgery, they got the blood report. The patient had AB-Negative group of blood with 7gm of haemoglobin which caused anxiety in Uma. But AB negative blood was not available in the blood banks.

"Madam! Please be kind enough to treat her. If you don't treat her, she will die. Madam! We trust you completely. You are a personification of God. That is why you have agreed to treat her. We are poor, uneducated and helpless. Madam! Do your best. Should anything happen to her, we will deem it to be her destiny." As the wailing parents were about to fall at her feet Uma stopped them and tried to calm them.

"Madam, when are you going to operate on my daughter Divya? Won't it be risky for the mother and the baby if it is further delayed?" asked Divya's mother, anxiety expressed through every syllable.

"As soon as I am done operating on this patient who is in a critical condition, I shall take up Divya's case," answered

Uma, walking up to Divya

"It is alright madam. I am getting mild pains only. I understand that that woman needs to be operated upon urgently. Please attend her first" said Divya. Uma gently pressed Divya's hand in appreciation.

"Patient's blood group is AB negative and her haemoglobin is 7gms. She is having profuse bleeding, certainly warrants blood transfusion, but we have not been able to procure it from any of the blood banks. None of the attendants has the same blood group. I am a bit hesitant to operate without keeping blood ready, but I am afraid, delaying surgery is a bigger risk" Uma explained to the anaesthetist who had just arrived. She was in a dilemma

"We will proceed with the surgery, though it is risky" Uma took a decision and instructed that the patient be shifted to the operation theatre.

Just then Divya's mother approached her to tell that Divya wanted to have a word with her. Uma's heart sank as she thought that Divya might have changed her mind and wanted to be taken care of first owing to her arrival at the hospital before the other patient and hers being a risky pregnancy too.

"Madam, I called my brother. He is about to leave the blood bank. If you could send her blood sample to the blood bank, he will get it matched with the blood reserved for me and get the same for her. I overheard what you said to the anaesthetist. She needs it more than I do. It is kept ready for me as a precautionary measure. I may or may not need it, but for her it is unavoidable. Please go ahead with her surgery, Madam!." Divya's empathetic words brought tears to Uma's eyes.

Overcome with emotion, she bent down and planted a kiss on Divya's forehead.

CHAPTER TWO

The Flower Garden

Bharathi felt like a wilted plant in the flower garden. She wandered listlessly among the plants gazing aimlessly into the darkness enveloping the world. The touch of each plant aggravated the hurt inside her.

Yes, these plants were his devoted offerings to her.

A bond of many years! Each plant in the garden had been his gift, personally tended by him. Each one of them was a symbol of love, affection and adoration...years have gone by.... Bharathi went down her memory lane.

Those were the first days of her medical practice. She was getting to adjust to her new environment. It was a place, a curious mix of both urban and rural. People were just getting to know her as a doctor.

Late one-night Sitaram brought his wife to her hospital in a critical state of eclampsia. She was already denied treatment in two private hospitals, as her condition was precarious.

Sitaram approached Bharathi with scepticism whether she agrees to treat her at all, and even if she agrees, what would be the amount of money she might demand in advance.

He was visibly agitated. But, to his surprise, Bharathi started treatment immediately without any demands and instilled hope in him. She consoled him and promised to save the patient. He looked upon her as the goddess of mercy.

Sitaram felt that her continuous attention and services, till the patient was out of danger, were unprecedented and rare. When his wife, of whose survival he has given up all hope, was out of danger, opened her eyes and spoke to him, Sitaram, overpowered with emotion, shed tears of joy.

"I don't know whether gods and goddesses exist; but this doctor-mother is a true goddess.", he declared repeatedly to his relatives and friends.

"Mother! This is a poor man's offering, I can't afford more" said Sitaram, humbly offering a little sum of money when his wife was discharged.

"Don't bother. She survived. That is enough", she said. Sitaram folded his hands, bowed to her in gratitude and reverence and took leave.

With the birth of a son, Sitaram, who had been a tiller of his one acre of land in his village, developed new ideas and plans. Selling away his land, he migrated to the town, obtained a vacant plot three streets away from Bharathi's hospital on lease and started a Nursery of plants.

It was mainly his concern for immediate and better medical care for his son and wife, that made him leave his native village and settle down in the town.

On January first, accompanied by his wife and son, Sitaram, greeted Bharathi with a large bouquet of roses from his nursery. Bharathi admired the roses of different colours with beaming eyes. Sitaram enthusiastically narrated his nursery and described the wide variety of plants he had collected.

"Mother! Kindly come to your house-front once." His insistence made her move along with him. Roses and chrysanthemums in galore of pots were a feast to the eyes.

"How beautiful!", Bharathi exclaimed in delight. Her transparent joy and the glow in her eyes pleased Sitaram.

"From my nursery Mother", He said with a touch of pride.

"They are marvellous! I cannot describe how awesome they are!" she touched the flowers as if she is touching the tender cheeks of newborn kids. She felt that her childhood came back to her.

"These flower pots are for you Madam", Sitaram's wife, Lakshmi, said with a broad smile.

"Really", Bharathi touched the hand of Lakshmi in a gesture of friendliness.

"Yeah! Mother! They are for you only. Please ask your compounder to pour water and take care of the plants regularly. I will also be here and take care whenever I find some time." said Sitaram, appealing to Bharathi. While leaving the flower pots there, he was appearing like a father leaving his daughter with her in-laws.

"I am busy in the nursery. I have manual work to do and attend to the many buyers who visit the nursery. Trust me, I don't have a single minute of leisure" he added with a tinge of happiness and pride.

Bharathi was happy to have the flowerpots adorning her house front, but she had qualms about accepting them without paying. "Would he be hurt if I offer him money?" She was hesitant.

Just then "Dr Anand", Bharathi's husband arrived. Sitaram had been wary of Dr Anand's serious demeanour. He caught hold of his wife's hand and stepped aside on seeing Dr Anand.

"Did you see the flowerpots? Aren't they splendid? " Bharathi asked.

"Yes"' Anand quipped without even glancing at them and went inside. Bharathi didn't expect a better response from him. She turned to Sitaram with a smile.

'Sitaram! I am extremely happy today. When I was a child, we had many flower plants in our back yard, and I used to nurture them personally. When I moved to town for my higher studies, I lost the divine touch and feel of plants.

Now, as you see, all my time is spent with hospital and household work" There was some regret and grief in her tone that she was missing things of beauty and joy in her daily routine. Sitaram could sense her feelings.

"Madam! Don't worry. From hereafter, I will see that a lot of flowers feast your eyes." said Sitaram.

"Sitaram! If you don't mind, keep this small amount", still hesitant, Bharathi stretched her hand forward.

"Madam! Are you giving me money? How can I sell my plants to you" asked Sitaram with shock and surprise?

"Sitaram! You have grown them for selling and your family is dependent on that income. How can I have so many of them without payment?", she tried to plead.

"Madam! You gave life to me and my son. But for you, we wouldn't be here like this today. If you had insisted for huge payment on that day our small piece of land would have been out of our possession, and this nursery would not have existed at all. It was your kindness which is supporting our survival" Bharathi is moved by Lakshmi's words.

This is a new experience for her. No one else has acknowledged her help so profoundly.

Pure and simple, this gesture of Sitaram and his wife touched her heart and stirred her feelings of sublimity. Their affection and love strengthened her beliefs and affirmed her faith in humanity.

"Look, Lakshmi! It was after all my duty and part of my work..." Before Bharathi completed her sentence, Lakshmi intervened, "This is also part of our routine work Mother!"

"No. No...You have to spend so much of money from your pocket for fertilizers, pesticides etc. apart from the time and energy you invest...", Bharathi was reluctant to accept the plants as a gift.

"Please don't say like that Mother. We won't accept any money from you" said Sitaram with an air of finality and walked away grabbing his wife's hand.

Sitaram took care of the plants that were gifted to Bharathi regularly. He used to replace some of the plants which shrivelled, checked each plant whether it was healthy and gave necessary instructions to the compounder.

The compounder, who didn't have any love for plants, considered it as an extra burden of work and tended to neglect them, One day Sitaram came to see the plants.

"Aww! This plant has withered. Is there a scarcity of water?" Sitaram's wailing irritated the compounder.

"What is the matter, man! Just because a plant withers a little, you make a fuss over it and wail as though you have lost thousands of rupees"

"Life is more precious than thousands of rupees. You may not know this, but Doctor-mother and I know this. If you don't take proper care of the plants, I may have to report to madam!". Sitaram took on the compounder.

Bharathi overheard their conversation and warned the compounder. She firmly believes that a person should not die due to lack of food or proper healthcare. Her belief was reaffirmed by Sitaram's words regarding plants. She became sad with the realization that the present world, which is full of gaps, inequalities and injustices, does not allow this to happen.

As time flowed, Lakshmi had two more children, had imminent eclampsia both the times and escaped near miss death.

"Doctor-mother! We are indebted to you for many births to come, for what you have done for us.", said, Lakshmi prostrating at Bharathi's feet. Bharathi never relished such humble reverence from people. She caught Lakshmi's shoulders and lifted her.

"Hey! What are you doing? When did you learn these prostrations? O.K. What about the debt I owe you? How I should payback? Tell me"

"We are poor. How could you be indebted to us? Since years we are getting free treatment and medicines from you. If we were to pay for all that, we might not be having a single meal per day and wouldn't have survived this far. More than that, you gave us the courage to face the problems and challenges of life." Lakshmi's eyes were full of tears and her voice choked with emotion.

"Lakshmi! This is unfair. When you make calculations, they should be accurate. Since so many years I am enjoying the beauty and fragrance of flowers just because of you, without slightest effort or expenditure of any sort on my part. Now, make a proper calculation and tell me who owes to whom". Lakshmi wiped her eyes and smiled.

"Lakshmi! No doubt, in the present-day world, everything is measured in terms of money. But there are certain things of beauty and values which can't be measured with the scale of money. So, stop these calculations and go home happily" Lakshmi bowed silently and left.

Several years disappeared into the bosom of time. Bharathi is now unable to work round the clock as in the past. She had to make many compromises to save her marriage with a husband who doesn't cherish the values she loves and knows only vulgar spending but not earning by right means. She is bearing this trauma and continued to live according to her values.

There were a lot of changes in Sitaram's family too. His two sons didn't come up in life, his daughter's married life failed and returned to her parents' care along with two children. Not able to bear all this, Lakshmi's health deteriorated and died suddenly.

Apart from these crises, the nursery slowly declined in quality and quantity due to natural calamities and financial problems.

One day Sitaram came to Bharathi, tried to tell her something, but stopped hesitantly.

"What is the matter Sitaram? You are not to be seen for so many days. What happened?"

"Mother! I am somewhat unwell, nothing very serious of course" Sitaram murmured.

"Come. I will examine you and give some medicines" Bharathi examined him and gave him some medicines. Sitaram stood before her silently with bent head.

"What is it Sitaram! Tell me." She asked him with a surprise. She has known him as an ever cheerful, active and courageous man despite many setbacks in life. "Recent tragic incidents might have traumatized him.", she told herself.

"Mother! I want five hundred rupees urgently" his voice was slow and grief-stricken. She looked at him with disbelief. Sitaram didn't approach Bharathi for any help at any time even under the worst financial crisis. Even if she offered some help, he declined it gently, but firmly. She knew how much humiliation he might have felt to ask now.

"Sitaram! Come. Let us go home."

Sitaram walked behind Bharathi as in a dream. Bharathi gave him a cupful of cheese and went inside to get the money.

"Why did you take the money now?" queried Dr Anand, who was observing her.

"For Sitaram" Bharathi was hurt by his rude voice.

"Is this a charity organization to give money to any riff-raff on the street", Bharathi is worried that Sitaram might hear these words.

"Sitaram is asking money for the first time in his life. He must have asked me because there is no other way to solve his problem, Why do you abuse him unnecessarily?"

"Might be this is the first time, but not the last. Look at that fellow. He seems to have addicted to drink alcohol. From now on he will come to you with a tearful story and beg for money. Remember." Said Anand, who drinks heavily every night

"Sitaram is a good man with some values. A man who loves flowers and people, can't do vicious things" Bharathi pleaded though she knows pretty well that it is in vain.

"Selling flowers is his profession. A man can sell flowers and A.K. forty-seven guns also. His profession need not reflect his nature." His words were like stinging insects around her ears and beyond her forbearance.

She knows that Anand is demonstrating the attitude that would result if one fails to foster in his heart faith in humans, love and respect for fellow men, which required as much diligent care as the flower plants in one's garden.

Once again she realized that she failed utterly in fostering a flowering plant, if not a flower garden, in her husband's heart. Instead of ruminating over it, she thought it was her immediate duty to give the money to Sitaram and send him away with dignity and respect.

She rushed into the verandah only to know that Sitaram already left. Bharathi's heart sunk into deep grief. What an act of rudeness! ...What a heartless brutality!... She was wandering listlessly among the plants. Her heart was longing to grow and nurture flower gardens in many hearts.

(This story was selected as one of the best 12 stories out of around 1400 stories translated into English from almost all Indian languages, by Humanscape, a fortnightly magazine from Mumbai).

CHAPTER THREE

Break the Shackles

Purna discarded the book she was reading in disgust. Those who write these stories and articles are sidelining the most important issues for women! They are looking to brainwash women who think with a bit more freedom and attach more shackles to them according to plan.

How dare the writers of these articles state that because of women's freedom, self-sufficiency and her life outside the home are leading to the breakdown of the families? They are preaching the women to confine themselves to home to avoid the dire consequences of marital friction. Her mind was muddled and she tried to forget by dusting the books on the shelf.

After dusting the books and shelf, Purna felt fatigued and leaned on the sofa. Fatigue! Yes, it is extreme fatigue! ... But the fatigue is not due to exhaustion. Fatigue that comes with a relentless struggle, fatigue that comes with the struggle for existence, the struggle for survival, the struggle for food, the struggle for education and above all, the struggle for dignity.

Marriage was a big turning point in her life which made her face the struggles. Away from the magic of crazy dreams and sentiments, created by movies and literature, she never had a big sweet dream about marriage or a husband and had never got carried away by the world of imagination.

She had been seeing many men, including her father, since her childhood. Their mentalities may be different but with the same attitude of different magnitudes with regards to the treatment meted to their better halves.

She did not expect her husband to be any different. But, she had very mild hope that it would be nice if he were different. The foolish hope remained hidden and never surfaced.

That is why she, who used to reason, question and practice everything if it seemed right, felt offended when Suresh, her husband, despised her.

"Do not act as if you were descended from the sky. See your mom, my mom and learn how to behave! Learn what the place of a woman is" said her husband. Purna was surprised to hear him talking in such a harsh tone.

This man, who was not even twenty-five years old, was so rude and so mean towards women! He belonged to the modern generation, but modern only in physical appearance, following new fashions but unable to cultivate modern thinking.

"How can I be like my mom or your mom? Ours is a new generation. We need to have progressive and new ideas," Purna said with solemnity though she was hurt by his uncivilized behaviour.

She felt perturbed to see the displeasure in her husband's face. But it was against her nature to obey any command without reasoning. Their whole life was ahead. To live life long compromising with his thoughts and orders meant to remain as a living corpse.

The thought itself is unbearable...No, No. I should change his attitude. She understood that his sense of superiority was nurtured by the people around him. He blindly followed the oldfangled ideas rooted in this society.

She hoped that he would realize his mistake when she opened the door to new ideas. The feelings of the wife being a slave, maid or shadow, were outdated. He should be a friend, a companion, a friend who has to share the joys and sorrows, experiences, hardships, feelings and emotions.

She strongly believed that a husband should be a companion and a friend to share the joys, sorrows, experiences, hardships, feelings and emotions.

'If I remain his slave, maid, or shadow and kill my warm imagination, reactions, and dignity, not only I but, he will also be the loser. He does not realize that incompatibility between partners would disturb the society as a whole in the long run. His reluctance to accept the change was making him behave in that manner. That's why he is trying to shut my mouth by force.' Purna was engrossed in her thoughts.

'It is not correct for you to talk like this. It is alright if you can't think for yourself. At least open your eyes and look around you. How fast the world is changing! "Purna's words sounded hollow to herself.

'The real world is changing rapidly physically, scientifically, and technologically. But human mentality, strongly entrenched in beliefs and ideas that were being carried on for many, many years, is not changing at the same pace.

The new ideas and notions did not move the men as intensely as they moved women leading to clashes between the couples. If he had changed along with me, he would have let me speak with freedom. Both of us would have exchanged ideas with love, would have shared fragrant friendship, and would have been absorbed with same emotions', thought Purna

Suresh got up angrily and left as he did not want to talk to her. The confrontation that had stopped then erupted again when he came to know that she had secured a job.

"Now you don't have to do the job. Whatever I earn is enough for the family... All you have to do is stay at home and tidy up the house and look after the children," he ordered.

'Why did he marry a woman with post-graduation when he thought he wanted a wife to look after the children and the house only? Is the educated wife a status symbol like a big house and an expensive car?' thought Purna inwardly.

"What you earn may be enough. But for me, the purpose of doing the job is not just for earning it is to boost my spirits, to prove my strengths, to use my intellect and talent for this society, to gain an identity for myself. All these things that I have mentioned are unattainable if I remain just your wife".These ideas were expressed by Purna aloud and boldly.

"Stop it! I hate to hear such dizzying words." Suresh's face, flushed with rage, became clumsy.

Purna also did not want to talk to him who lost his temper and discriminating power. She remained silent and joined the job the next day. When Purna returned home from office in the evening there was a big fight.

"Don't overreact with your unnecessary anger. I am not doing anything wrong. There are a lot of working women. Why do you say that I am acting against the world? "Purna asked patiently. Her calm and composed manner and argument further irritated him.

His ego was damaged by her defiance and in her taking up the job. He was boiling with anger.

Not shaken by his anger, looking straight into his eyes, Purna said with a clear and firm voice, "It is a waste of time and energy to argue on this issue. I can't sit at home without doing any job. Then let's leave this issue and think about how to live happily while doing our respective jobs".

She tried her level best to involve her husband in doing household chores but failed miserably.

"There is no gender for work. What we have named as male works or female works were formed by our ancestors centuries ago. Now we can change those gender roles and do all the works depending on our needs. Come, and grind these pulses now", Suresh looked at her as though he would bite her head off.

"Conceiving and delivering a child and breastfeeding are the only things men can't do. Everything else can be done by both males and females. Come on, let us prepare this snack" Purna insisted on him in extending his help in cooking on one holiday. But he didn't oblige and all her talk was like talking to a brick wall!

Purna's hope to change him with persuasion or entreat or provoking or instigating was futile. She then decided to turn a deaf ear to his abusive words.

She dedicated all her energies to the household work and office work without getting hassled. After the birth of her daughter and son, her burden of work doubled.

Yet, Suresh kept grumbling on some pretext or other. He was always in complaining mode with persistent chiding that the house was not clean, children not tidy or the cooking was unappetizing. Without any hesitation, he linked all happenings to the fact that she had taken up a job.

When Suresh was studying for his competitive exams, while offering him tea and snacks, she flipped through the books and got interested to study and appear for the exams.

When her husband was successful in the exams Purna was overwhelmed with joy. When he got a good job after passing the exam, she felt elated and instantly prepared a good dinner for him and his friends to celebrate the occasion. She was too glad when he was congratulated and appreciated.

In spite of being overburdened with the increased load of work, Purna prepared for her exams. Though she was not satisfied with her preparation, she appeared for the examination and got through successfully.

She announced the good news to Suresh with great pleasure. But he didn't utter even a single word of appreciation, pretended as if he didn't hear her words. Her excitement vanished as she noticed his noncommittal attitude. Although everyone else applauded her talent, she was scorned by her husband.

He has no sense of 'us' except 'his'. When a marriage lacks the sense of 'us', how much chaotic it can become, was being experienced by Purna. Job responsibilities increased along with the salary increase. Sometimes she was compelled to work in the office for long hours

Purna performed her duties at the workplace with the utmost care and enthusiasm as she was getting ample opportunity to exhibit her talents.

While climbing the steps of success, she was deprived of the support, approval and happiness from her husband. When someone praised her ingenuity, agility, and talent, he shrugged and diverted the conversation. This hurt Purna a lot.

She was receiving laurels from the outside world, but the blatant apathy of her husband made her feel very depressed.

When someone praises her ingenuity, agility, and talent, he shrugs and diverts the conversation to something else. Though she is receiving laurels from the outside world, blatant apathy of her husband made her feel so depressed.

Self consoling, comforting, patting her back, taking the reins of slipping courage and self-confidence into her hand, she moved forward.

But that did not help for long. Jealousy had already added to the arrogance inherent in him. Now suspicion had even begun. When he passed the exams and got promotions, he proudly said that he got it because of his intelligence and talent.

But he didn't accept that the same thing applied to Purna also. He hit on her self -respect with a cruel argument that women can't be successful in their careers unless they lose their chastity.

He took her every movement and every word negatively. Suresh appears very refined to the outsiders. No one ever believes that there is an animal inside him which comes out and attacks her frequently.

Between Purna, who wanted her opinions, her ideas and feelings to be valued and Suresh, who wanted his authority to prevail always without contradiction, arose constant conflicts.

Whenever there was a fight, he would throw a suitcase and three to four saris in front of her and shout, "Get out of my house!" She used to wonder how this educated man could talk in such a shameless manner. How could this man attempt to throw out the woman whom he married, promising that he would live with her and protect her lifelong?

Purna always thought that everything in the house including the building belonged to both of them, though the lion's share of the monetary contribution was hers. She felt humiliated whenever he shouted, "Get out of my house".

But she used to control her anger thinking that if she also talked and acted in haste, her marriage would certainly be ruined. She did not want her children to get affected by their parents' ignorance and stupid decisions. She used to behave with utmost tolerance, though her heart was burning

"He is getting out of control because you are not reacting. If you retort, he will come to his senses." Purina's sister-in-law, who had noticed conflicts between them, Commented.

'Thinking power should bestow the person wisdom and discernment, replying back right and left might reduce my anger and resentment, doesn't solve the problem. But doesn't a responsible, high-rank officer know such small things about life?' thought Purna.

Gradually, it had come to a point when she could not bear to hear his scornful words any more. One day When Suresh warned her angrily to select only one of the two, 'her career or family', she was stunned.

'What crime did I commit to provoke him to talk so rudely? Does he have the authority to speak like this just because he is a husband and a man? Why should I choose either career or family? I want both. My life would be incomplete if I choose only one of them.'

"Do you know how inappropriately you are talking? Why should I choose one of the two, career or family? "She asked. Suresh's face was burning with rage.

"If you want to wander outside well dressed, without taking care of home and children, why do you want children and family, you can as well hang on your to 'great' job." She could gauge the sarcasm in his tone.

"You are unjustly slandering me. Do you care a tenth of what I care about the house and the children? How can you corner me like this when you are enjoying rights only and not at all shouldering any responsibility what so ever", asked Purna

"Don't boast that you are doing a great job! Except running like a machine, are you spending your time leisurely with your children? "Are you helping them in their academics?' screamed Suresh

"I work for 17-18 hours a day, running around like a machine. Even then time is not enough to do the things. Yet, I am allocating little quality time for the children to make them feel happy and secure. Where is enough time to gossip leisurely?'

'Perhaps his demand might be that the time I spend on the job should also be spent on the children and him. If I stop doing the job, his ego might get satisfied, He never accepts that he could climb every step of his career without much effort, without the responsibility of the family because of my full cooperation. When I am trying to climb the ladder on my own, with great difficulty and without any help from anywhere, he is pulling my legs down.'

"Well, I am not taking any responsibility for children's education and not organizing the family in an ideal way. Okay, I agree. But you're so smart and intelligent, you can as well use some of your time at home for the kids, instead of limiting the non-office hours to your enjoyment and your growth. Why don't you do that?" Purna asked him as gently as possible.

Suresh didn't expect this type of cool reaction from her. He thought that she would react with fear or anger when she was warned to select one of the options between career and family. He was infuriated

"Don't be over smart. Now you decide whether you want your career or children and me. If you want family, resign your job, keep your mouth shut and confine yourself to the home. If you prefer to do a job, get out of my house, now, I say, right now" Suresh shouted at her, opened the steel cupboard, pulled out a bunch of saris and threw them on her face.

Instead of getting angry by his obscene behaviour, she pitied him for his ignorance. She did not forget that she was not the only one in such misery, and that ninety per cent of husbands like him were worse than him. Hence she showed much restraint.

"In a mood of rage, you are forgetting what is good and what is bad. Please cool down. Think calmly. This house, these children, your job and my job, belong to both of us. If we think in a divergent and selfish way, the result will be disastrous" Purna tried to convince him. But, he reacted with unnecessary fury.

"Are you teaching me morals? Get out! "He grabbed her arm very firmly and pulled her out of the bedroom. She was thunderstruck by his behaviour. She was afraid that the children might notice this ugly scene.

"What is this? Leave me', she cried. So far his indecent behaviour was limited to words and body language, now it had turned physical. She freed herself from his clutches and tried to go back into the bedroom.

Then he pushed her with rage, her forehead hit the door frame and blood-spattered around. The wounded mind, the blow on the forehead had forced her to make the most important decision now, though she was trying to pacify him with all the possible, peaceful ways so far.

"I have decided. I want my family and career, both. Now you have to decide. If you accept my decision, we will stay together happily. If you don't want to accept, it is up to you, but then, you have to get out of this house, not me." Purna said firmly, controlling her exploding emotions, agitation, grief and rage.

"How arrogant you are!" Purna restrained enraged Suresh with her hands.

'With the ego that he is a man, that he has authority, with the courage that I am not equal to him in physical strength, he is attacking me. But, he doesn't know that if I want, I can repel his physical attack. But I don't want to do such a stupid, barbaric thing.' Purna's body was trembling with anger

"Enough. Your behaviour, which is already uncivilized and uncultured, is disgusting now. Don't get down any further. Don't talk unnecessary rubbish. You had yelled at me many times and asked me to get out of the house. But I restrained myself from reacting so far to avoid disturbance in our family. Now I can't tolerate your absurd behaviour any more. This is my house. Get out", Purna said with a stern voice.

Exploded with anger, he scolded her with mean and uncivilized words, packed a few clothes in the suitcase and rushed out of the house.

What happened next is a series of events that she hated to recollect again. It is true that Purna did not lose her self confidence because of them, but became very stubborn and faced everything with courage. "What else do I lose?" She faced life with a detached attitude and courage.

"May I come in?" Purna got out of her thoughts when she heard the voice of Surendra, Suresh's friend, as he dropped his sandals near the door.

"Please come", she said to him.

"Have you read the book I gave?" Surendra asked, turning the pages of the English women's magazine on the tea pod.

"I read. The magazine in your hand also has stories and articles about women. I read them also".

"What is your comment?" Surendra looked curious.

"The summary of the content in the book you gave and this magazine is the same. As times have changed, so the females are allowed to go out of the house, can study as long as the father allows, can do the job as long as the father or the husband allows. She should stop doing the job when not allowed.

Even if she does the job, the authority on her earning is her husband or father. It is better if she does a part-time job to look after her husband, children and home. For women, husband, children and family are important, but 'career' is not at all that important.

If someone prefers a career also along with the family, she would be threatened that she might have to lose her husband, family, or even the children." Surendra was listening to her critical analysis silently.

" Women, who chose 'career' as the main focus of their lives after listening to the teachings of feminists in the Western world who advocated 'women's freedom' and 'women's emancipation' etc. are now regretting for not having marriage, family and children and for their lives being incomplete.

Feminists in our country should also learn from the experiences of western women and recognize the misfortunes that can arise if they prioritize 'career'.

In our culture, it is ingrained in our minds that women should have the family as the sole priority and thus protect the marriage system and family system from destruction.

This is what is written in these magazines and books, isn't it? Or did I went wrong in understanding these articles?" she paused as if she is waiting for his answer

"What you understood is correct. The fact is that yours is a straight answer while they were all beating around the bush"

"That is what my problem is. My words and deeds are straight forward, which is unpalatable for some people", Purna smiled

"By the way, why did you give this book to me? The matter in this book deftly argues to sidestep women's issues? It is a different matter to say that a woman should not ruin her marriage with haste, rage and rudeness. She should behave with discretion, responsibility and restraint.

But to a woman who thinks independently, wants to have happy married life as well as bright career, is it not brutal to threaten her by saying that your freedom and career are the causative factors for the destruction of marriage system?" asked Purna with anguish

"Your thinking power is great. But, are you not aware of the damage caused by your separation from Suresh? Even your children might blame you in future for keeping them away from their father and for not adjusting with their father at least for their sake."

After hearing his words Purna started to think. "Maybe it is true that children might find me guilty in future. I know, the violence, humiliation, and grief I have experienced may seem insignificant to them. Their father, who stayed away from them, might seem precious. But showing the pretext of the children, Surendra is suggesting me to compromise. He wants me to regret the mistake I did not make."

"I can understand the anxiety you have to restore our family. But who is to blame for our breakup?" Purna asked with a calm

"Leave it. There is no point in digging into what happened. I just want the two of you to be back together".

Purna is thinking." How to come together! Only when his views about women and wife change, when he treats his wife with love and respect, at least tolerate her, then, there is a possibility of thinking to live together. "

"When necked out from the home, if there is another man in the place of Suresh, he would have gone into a very wrong path.

But look at Suresh! He is willing to compromise with you when I tried to convince him. You should feel happy about that".

Surendra's words filled Purna with indignation and rage. What a fine judgment by this man! Purna's face flushed with resentment.

She very curtly asks Surendra to leave her place.

Purna continues to fight and break the shackles which are stifling her freedom, which are destroying her self-respect, and which are roadblocks for her chance to live in dignity and sobriety.

* * *

CHAPTER FOUR

Quagmire

A feeling as if the brain is exploding, a pain as if the heart is fragmenting into pieces. Shailaja quivered on seeing her daughter Swecha there and in such condition. She trembled with a storm of grief that engulfed her.

Swecha was lying semiconscious on the dirty, stinking floor in the cellar of the apartment complex. Shailaja ran towards Swecha, took her daughter on the lap and shuffled her blood-soaked clothes properly and covered her half-naked body with her sari. With her mother's touch, Swecha opened her eyes slowly and observed the surroundings around her and uttered confused words.

Soon after she could recognize her mother's face and tremble as a tender leaf, hugged her mother tightly and began weeping with gasping sobs. Shailaja took her daughter onto her chest and consoled her gently patting her back and tried to control her own anxiety and grief.

•

Sailaja left for her office in the morning and Swecha, packing her lunch box, rushed to the college before her mother. When Swecha had not returned home by late evening, Shailaja got worried and asked all her friends she knew about her whereabouts. None of them knew where

Swecha was. Shailaja was tensed up and was a bundle of nerves. As her husband was out of the city, her worry shot up, and she felt that she was between the devil and deep blue sea.

Usually, Swecha informs her mother If she is unable to reach home in time. 'Why didn't she call and tell me that she will be late. She never had the habit of leaving home or staying outside for a long time without informing me. Did Swecha go to the birthday party of a friend who is unknown to me? Did she go to the hotel or to watch a movie with her friends? Is she tangled up in traffic!' Many thoughts were running through Shailaja's mind when a phone call disturbed her thoughts.

Her heart skipped when an unknown person by name Neelima, called her from Swecha's phone and gave her the information about her whereabouts.

As per the address given by Neelima, Shailaja rushed to the apartment complex which was located at city outskirts. Neelima was waiting for her at the in-gate.

Neelima was moving anxiously to and fro from cellar to the in-gate of the apartment complex while following up the call to know how far Shailaja had reached. As soon as she got off her cab, Neelima, after making sure that it was Shailaja, headed towards the cellar.

Shailaja, who was walking along with her, trembled with fear as many evil thoughts occupied her mind. 'Did anyone kidnap Swecha and captivated her here? Did anyone harm her? ...Is she alive?'....It seemed as if someone had taken away all her strength.

She felt weak in the knees. She was about to fall, controlled herself and grabbed Neelima's hand tightly. Radhika, who was walking silently engrossed in her thoughts, looked at Shailaja with pity as she held her hand for support.

"Please be brave. We have come closer" Neelima said softly consoling Shailaja.

"I returned from the office and was parking the car. Then I noticed the girl lying there. I ran fast and checked that she was breathing well and there are bruises and blood on her neck. I thought of waking her up and taking her to the hospital. But it was difficult for me to move her, singlehanded. I got some courage when I found her phone lying there. There were many missed calls from your mobile. Immediately I called you. I was so much relieved when you picked up the phone. There! Your girl is there".

Shailaja tried to cope with the grief and anxiety engulfing her. She thanked Neelima for not ignoring her daughter and taking up the responsibility of informing her without thinking about the dire consequences and the legal hassles if something went wrong.

•

"Our flat is right here on the fourth floor. Let's go to our flat first. Let's try to find out what happened to Swecha. If required, we will take her to the doctor." Neelima gave support to Sailaja to lift her up from the floor. Then the two of them lifted Swecha, held her together on both the sides and led her to Neelima's flat.

Sailaja was pondering why did Swecha come to this apartment complex and that too, to this foul-smelling, semi-dark cellar? None of their relatives or friends was staying in this complex which was far away from their home, then what made her come to this place? Are any of Swecha's friends staying here?... Shailaja walked along with Neelima, controlling her agony, hugging her daughter and covering her body, feeling ashamed of her condition.

THE WAR

Meanwhile, Neelima got a call from her mother-in-law telling her about the nuisance going on in the next-door flat. After getting off the lift, Shailaja was astonished to see the scene in the flat near the lift through the opened doors. She found Swecha's friend Anusha and three other girls lying on the sofa semi-conscious, talking nonsense, giggling and singing in a vulgar manner.

Seeing Swecha, one of the girls came out rushing and pulled her rudely and strongly. Shailaja and Neelima, who felt shocked for a moment, forcibly released Swecha from the clutches of that girl and brought her to the adjoining flat which belonged to Neelima

Swecha was not in a position to say what had happened to her. Based on the situation in the flat where the girls were staying and by what Neelima's mother-in-law said, they could imagine what was going on there.

•

Anusha had lost her mother. She was being raised by a single parent, her father. Anusha's father was out of town. Swecha and her friends had skipped college in the afternoon and were in Anusha's flat. They all were partying and were under the influence of alcohol and drugs.

The residents in the remaining five flats in that floor, elders coming back from the offices and children from their schools and colleges, tolerated the disturbance for a while, tried to control them as they were creating a nuisance with songs, dances, loud noises and screams, but hesitated to report to the police in the absence of Anusha's father, Vikram. He moved to this flat recently and was friendly with all of them. They took Vikram's contact number from the Apartments' club office and informed him about the happenings. He requested them to forgive his daughter and

• 42 •

that he would be reaching home within a few hours

Shailaja recalled that when Anusha was a toddler, her mother left her husband and daughter, and her father took care of Anusha without remarrying. Swecha brought her friend on and off to stay with them for two to three days, as Anusha was feeling lonely and sometimes depressed. Shailaja did not enquire anything about Anusha other than listening to what Swecha told about her.

No matter how affectionately her father took care of, Anusha was not able to bear the situation. As she was deprived of her mother's love, affection, touch, care and security, she might have been in a vulnerable state and slipped into the trap of such vices.

'But what had happened to Swecha? Why is she in such an awkward position?'Sailaja could not understand the reason for her daughter's distressing condition

Swecha's parents raised her without any restrictions or hegemonic pressures. Setting lofty goals, they encouraged & motivated her always to achieve her goals. They taught the children that there are no short cuts to success and that success can be achieved through hard work only.

Uday, their son, who believes in this principle, is an academically brilliant student and is now researching at Harvard University. Born eight years after Uday, Swecha was too pampered by her parents. Shailaja wanted her daughter to become doctor, Swecha said that she had no interest in medicine and that she would do a law course. Shailaja didn't' want to impose her wish and allowed Swecha to go ahead according to her passion.

Swecha joined in the Law Institute two months back and dreamt of becoming one of the Best Lawyers.

Swecha never misused the freedom she had. At such a young age, she behaved with so much of maturity, which sometimes surprised her mother as well.... Shailaja was in deep thoughts.

She was wiping the blood off Swecha's body and cleaning the wounds by dipping the handkerchief in the hot water brought by Radhika. She was unable to understand how Swecha got hurt. She had many unanswered questions

"Did anyone force Swecha to have alcohol and drugs? In this attempt, did these girls attack Swecha when they had no control over themselves? Why was Swecha found unconscious in the cellar? Has anyone physically or sexually abused Swecha?"

Shailaja saw the other girls in Anusha's flat while she was collecting Swecha's clothes. For the first time in her life, her thoughts were filled with fear as she looked at the girls who had been drinking and taking drugs. She had never dreamt of seeing her daughter among those who were addicted to alcohol and drugs. All her beliefs and values seemed to be crumbling.

"Take your daughter to the doctor first. I will take tackle these girls until Anusha's father arrives." Said Neelima after offering water and a cup of Coffee. She helped Shailajato take swecha in a cab to Dr Shruti's Hospital.

After admitting her there, slowly Swecha regained her full consciousness. She was engulfed in grief while she was coming into her senses. She was afraid of looking into her mother's eyes.

'How shocked mom must have been to see me in this condition!' She could not bear the thought that this incident had destroyed mom's faith in her. She knew that her mom was always with her in every step she

She never spied on her like her friends' moms. She never imposed on her to follow her footsteps though she was more experienced and more accomplished. She knew what was good for Swecha. She always used to listen to her with patience and always accepted Swecha's point of view.

'My loving mother has to face this miserable situation unnecessarily, though I am not involved in this terrible incident. I should tell mom everything that had happened to me until I lost consciousness.' thought Swecha.

Anusha had called her while she was in class. She was crying and informed her that her father went out of town and that she was very much upset, feeling too lonely and that she wanted to commit suicide. Swecha warned her friend not to have such foolish thoughts and immediately took permission from her lecturer and went to Anusha's place.

By the time Swecha reached Anusha's house, Anusha and her friends were there in the flat. They were already drinking alcohol and taking drugs. Noticing that the situation was not normal, she wanted to go back. But Anusha's friends tried to stop her and forced her to drink alcohol.

While trying to escape from them, they pulled her, ripped off her shirt, chased Swecha, who was running in fear, not knowing in which direction she was going. They caught hold of Swecha and forcefully made her drink alcohol. After that, she didn't remember anything that happened to her.... After listening to her daughter's plight, Shailaja felt as if all her energy was sucked out

Shailaja briefly told Dr Shruti about the entire incident. Has there been a sexual assault on Swecha in the cellar, and if so, what should be done to prevent her from suffering physically and mentally? Should a police report be filed? ... Shailaja questioned Shruti with vague thoughts.

"Let's revive Swecha first. We will talk with Anusha and her friends and find out more details about the incident.

We will consult a lawyer for advice on filing a police complaint.... You have to be brave." Shruti tried to console Shailaja.

"No matter how hard I try to be brave, I'm not able to cope madam! Drugs and Alcohol are lucrative businesses attracting the mafia. Those greedy and unscrupulous people are making the liquor and drugs available for even high school students who are lured to these habits.

Liquor is available in all places, including the places very close to schools and temples. Drugs are as easily available in colleges and universities as chocolates. The liquor mafia and the drug mafia empire is spreading rapidly across the borders of countries, states, cities and even into the villages. We are reading in newspapers and listening in TV channels with prominent titles like " The city is in intoxication", "Youth in the clutches of drugs" etc., but never bothered about the issues, as they didn't touch us so far...Sailaja was telling Sruthi in remorse filled voice.

Shruti looked at Shailaja sympathetically saying that she was repenting for the detachment of people like her.

. 'What can ordinary people like us do?'Sailaja thought. Quickly she picked up self-confidence, and thought, 'Can't we do something? History has proven that the extraordinary sacrifices of ordinary people can lead to revolutionary changes!

"I did not believe when my friends told me that it has become common for such parties to take place in houses of certain sections of people. Now I understand that the time is not too far away for such parties reaching our houses as well....The utter failure of the regulatory authorities or the nexus between them and the liquor and drug mafia... whatever it may be, the end result is that our children are becoming victims.' Sailaja paused for a while

'Now my fear and grief are not just about my daughter Doctor!, but about all the children like Swecha. Should I keep quiet and neglect even now and leave it aside as before? Should we not take this matter seriously?" Shailaja Questioned herself with boundless agony.

CHAPTER FIVE

The Path

Sharada's mind is in turmoil like a raging sea. It started with fierce thunder and lightning, with hailstones piercing the ears. Karunya, who said he was going to a music concert with his friends in the evening, hurriedly started the car and left without answering even when asked at what time he would be home.

Sharada is alarmed about Karunya when the headwind started. It is unknown where the music concert is conducted and at what time it ends. She is not sure whether Karunya comes home, or goes to the movie with his friends, or whether he went to a music concert or spending time with his friend's elsewhere!

Sandeep, Koundinya, Rahmat, Karunya's friends, who come home on and off, do not appear to be having bad habits. But, sometimes what is seen may not be true! She does not know what kind of friends her son is having outside, whom she has not seen!

From the time he joined in college, she is worried about her son, with whom he is befriending, whether he is making friends with a good-natured friend who doesn't have any vices, where he is moving about etc. until he came home,

'Children need to be trusted. You shouldn't suspect them every moment. If Karunya comes to know your doubts, he might feel insulted. He will grow properly and reach higher goals if he is allowed to live with enough freedom" lectured Rajesh, her husband.

'Don't I know the benefits of raising children with freedom, without any restrictions, pressures or surveillance? What about the attractions and addictions which are pulling the sensitive teens so forcibly?

In which direction the modern technological innovations, cell phones, internet, social media, WhatsApp, etc., are leading the youth? Where is the control of the evil that can happen?' with the sound of the message in the cell, Sarada came out of her thoughts

It was two o'clock, past midnight. Karunya has not yet come. 'He could have informed me. He knew that she would not close her eyes and sleep until he returns home.

Till recent times, his whole world is around me, he used to refuse to go anywhere leaving me. Even when I told him to go for school excursions paying money every time, and see different places along with his friends with a thought that it would be better if he experiences how to get along in the outside world, he used to refuse to leave me adamantly.

Then I used to think, why he is not mixing with friends? How would he develop an independent personality if he doesn't friendship with the kids ... Now he has transformed like this. When he was studying tenth class, he asked his father to buy the latest version of the Apple phone, but he refused to buy it.

Then he was very annoyed and went on fast till it is bought. While in Inter, he put out a tender for an expensive bike. Rajesh is too afraid of driving, that too, youngsters driving expensive bikes.

That is why he gave an ultimatum to his son that he wouldn't buy the bike at any cost. After a gap of six months again Karunya started pestering his father to buy a big expensive car.'

"Can we afford to buy an expensive car now? Just because both your mom and I are doing jobs, as we are not in the habit of spending so much on luxuries, we can maintain this style of living without much deficit. We can't afford to buy such expensive cars. Try to understand. " Rajesh tried to convince his son. But Karunya did not accept'

Rajesh bought a car that was a little cheaper than what he had finally asked for, as he was tired of trying to make his son realize. Sarada was also afraid about the possible consequences of her son's demand not getting fulfilled the possibility of running away from home or commit suicide in uncontrolled anger, to which the present youth are often vulnerable. So she also requested her husband to buy the car.

Although Sarada was fascinated to see Karunya learn to drive the car with agility in exactly fifteen days. She is confident of her son's driving skills but anxious with the thought that though he is driving safely in their presence, who knows, he may get stimulated by his hormones when he is with friends and might drive with rocket speed. If anything happens when he drives exceeding the speed limits! .....

New addictions and dangerous behaviours that are being practised in modern life, ordinary people like Sarada are horrified to hear and see driving with terrible speed, boundless eating and wasting food, vulgar exhibition of wealth, hanging on mobiles most of the time, committing violence, are added to the already existing misdemeanours or addictions continuing in the community from the past ... lying, stealing, smoking, alcohol, drugs, unhealthy Sexual behaviours etc. destroying the lives of young people. Sarada is too worried about the consequences.

Sarada Switched on the TV to divert her thoughts. On seeing the scene unfolding on the screen, she trembled. The son of a celebrity was killed in a head-on collision with a speeding car, killing three of his friends in the car and killing four others on the road on the spot, while two others were seriously injured.

The reporter says that the boy, who was around twenty years old, was driving under the influence of alcohol, failed to control the car due to excessive speed, and broke all the state-of-the-art safety equipment. Those scenes that are repeatedly shown on the channel are driving Sharada insane.

It seemed that all the grief the Parents, relatives and friends of the deceased might be experiencing, fell on her heart. With unbeknownst feeling her heart was pounding and her eyes were raining.

Suddenly another thing came to her mind. That celebrity son who made the accident is a senior student to Karunya in his college. Sharada rebuked her son when she found out that Karunya had a friendship with him.

'If we associate with the children of these neo rich people, we will get attracted to those their costly habits. What seems like luxuries to us are the minimum requirements for them. Sometime later they begin to appear to us also as necessities. We want everything they have. Do we need such friendships?!'

'My darling! Don't run after these ridiculous funs. Our legs should be strong on the ground. You have to set the highest goals and you have to aim for them, " requested Sarada, who represents the average middle-class mother.

Meanwhile, an idea came like a flash and Sharada's whole body was sweating. 'Is Karunya one of the other three in the car who died ?!' She is like a flying dry leaf flying in a whirlwind.

Then the phone rang. With a palpitating heart, Sharada picked up the phone with a hope that Karunya might have called. When she heard that the call is from the police station, she felt as though she is lost her senses.

Sharada, who was under the influence of the scenes seen on TV earlier, was a little bit happy when she found out that her son was alive. When she was told that Karunya had been arrested from the other side, she woke up her sleeping husband and handed the phone to him.

A mild fear is lurking in Sarada's mind for the past few months. They are leading a simple, modest and dignified life without any negative criticism from anyone so far. She became frightened, Karunya, with his new attractions, might land in dangerous situations which might force them to bow their heads. Her fears became a reality.

Rajesh, who considers talking loudly, leave alone conflict or confrontation as disrespectful, had to go to the police station. Sharada saw her husband crooked sadly dressed solemnly. Sharada looked at Rajesh who is wearing the shirt with a serious gaze. With the fear that she might have to hear very bad news, she remained silent with a dejected face.

While going out of the house Rajesh said that Karunya and his friends were arrested on the charge of driving under the influence of alcohol. Rajesh contacted his lawyer friend Srivastava and went to the police station along with him.

Sharada, sat on the doorstep when her husband left. Her brain was filled with thoughts of suffocation. After getting married, she had three miscarriages in a row. After many tests and treatments around the doctors, she conceived twins.

Till the ninth month of pregnancy, there were repeated scans, medications, bed rest ... at last, the twins were delivered by cesarean section after entering safety zone. But one of the twins, who was under-weight, died within a week after birth with pulmonary complication.

The survivor of the twins, Karunya, was not spoiled by over pampering by his parents, but, was cared with love and affection and suitable norms.

Believing that children need to be raised in an environment that provides the security and protection and that the parents should build an intimacy with the children, which can alleviate many of the doubts and anxieties that plague them, they nurtured Karunya accordingly.

Until the tenth standard, Karunya used to share with his parents, especially with his mother, whatever had happened in his school. He used to describe the interesting stories about his friends' antics, mischief, and their parents. He used to ask their opinion on every important matter and take the advice of his father before taking any decision.

Gradually, they noticed that he was moving away from them, that a thin screen seemed to slip between them. They saw it as a positive aspect, a part of his natural process of healthy growth. They are trying to lead an ideal life to become role models for their son.

Sarada was surprised to see that Karunya get such a good rank in the entrance examination for engineering despite his love for cricket, movies and music and didn't study with hectic pace even before the exams.

When his mother questioned him, 'Wouldn't it be better to read a little more and get a better rank?' he looked at her with a mischievous smile

Sarada noticed that Karunya is moving further away from them when he joined in engineering college. She is worried, with a thought, where his friendships and fun are heading. Rajesh, who doesn't express like his wife, also has that concern.

Though he warns his wife not to get over-concerned, he is observing his son's friends and enquiring their family background.

Where he is going with his friends, when is he returning home, how is he behaving in the college, whether he is behaving against their family values in or outside the college, whether he is addicted to alcohol, drugs, etc., whether he is involved in cine fans conflicts or the mad fights of caste, religion and region and whether he is in the gangs that are harassing the girls, in the name of love.

Rajesh occasionally warns Karunya that it is foolish not to use intelligence properly and to the maximum potential. Merely having an engineering degree is equal to a scrap paper in this most competitive world, if knowledge and appropriate skills are not acquired.

"If you spend the time enjoying every day and throughout the day, what is the meaning and value of that enjoyment? Don't lose your life by becoming a victim of vices that trapping the students very easily nowadays" Rajesh questions and warns his son, whenever he notices that his son is unnecessarily wasting his precious time on superfluous enjoyments.

Unable to control her anxiety, she was making calls to her husband repeatedly, He answered very briefly and hung up the phone.

The father and son came home with Srivastava at dawn. Karunya's eyes are puffy, he is walking like a dreamer, afraid to look straight at the mother's eyes. Avoiding his mother's concerned looks he went to his room. Rajesh's face is pale with extreme fatigue. He lowered his eyes and sat impatiently.

"Not much problem, Sarada! ..... There is no case. .... can I have some coffee? It has been a long time since I drank the coffee prepared by you, "Srivastava said, trying to ease Sarada's anxious look.

Sharada's heart was pounding as she did not know what had happened and what hassles her son is in, although she was a little relieved to have her son at home.

Before the music concert was over, Karunya and the other three friends went together to one of the rooms belonging to them. Karunya, a newcomer, drank alcohol under the pressure of his friends and senior students, who were addicted to alcohol and even spent the money their parents sent them for college fees and eventually exam fees.

Later, they wandered around in Karunya's car till midnight when they saw a car with girls passing by and chased it. Karunya was forced to go fast and cross the car by his friends who were yelling, screaming and whistling loudly.

Under the influence of alcohol, he could not control the car at increased speed and collided with the oncoming bike. The car and the bike were also badly damaged, but no fatal injuries were reported.

Srivastava was able to manage the case with his contacts in the police department. The police reprimanded, warned and forgave the first mistake and left Karunya and his friends. Karunya and his friends apologized, paid the money for the bike repair and promised not to make a similar mistake again.

* * *

Sarada and Rajesh were mentally depressed by the incident which caused a big shock. They wondered why and where the mistake was made. Despite being taken care of with so much attention and discipline, despite being observed with wide-open eyes, why Karunya fell into the abyss so pathetically?

They questioned themselves in deep despair. But, again, they were comforted with the realization that many young adults are influenced and impacted by the outside world more easily than the environment at home. In next moment they were worried about the future of their son.

Karunya, felt guilty to see the depressed faces of his parents, who were behaving normally, as though nothing has happened, restraining themselves from asking piercing questions. The experience of the police station taught him a great lesson. While at the police station, he was frightened by the sight of one of the accused being beaten up strongly.

How the police dealt with the criminals and the methods they followed to convict him made him creepy. The counselling, done skillfully by a police officer, before leaving Karunya, also had a profound effect on him. He began to evaluate his life with calm.

Karunya realized that he has been enjoying a comfortable, dignified life so far and was bothered about his desires and enjoyment only. He also realized that it is necessary to look around and beyond his life and understand and care about the lives of other people.

Standing firmly on the ground, he began to think about the destination he was to set, the direction he has to travel, though it may not be that easy to live in a different style, but might not be impossible.

He had a revelation that there is no opportunity either at college or at home to spend the profound energy produced by the hormones in his body at this age, and not knowing how to spend that energy, the resultant confusion is driving him for temporary thrills.

He had decided to divert his energy for constructive and beneficial activities, and not waste it on harmful activities

He shared his idea with ten close friends who were ready to move forward as soon as he received his call. Friends who like the idea got together in the evenings on college days and Sundays, met tenth graders and inter students in hostels, social welfare residential schools and colleges and offered assistance to improve their knowledge and skills, letting them know how valuable time and life are with examples of their life experiences.

Some of their pocket money is spent on the development and entertainment of those children. A new sparkle appearing on their face as they taste the joy of giving.

Sarada and Rajesh, who are busy with their job responsibilities, did not notice the turmoil in Karunya, the gradual transformation in him, the quiet work he and his friends are doing for those children who have fewer opportunities.

Although they seem to be more relaxed about their son than before, they still do not have a clear idea of his thinking and behaviour. Sarada's heart was pounding every time she heard about the youngsters who were falling prey to the vices.

* * *

One day Karunya asked both his parents to come with him without giving any details. Although the calmness and joy that had recently appeared on her son's face were satisfying to Sharada, something hesitancy and fear did not cease to torment her.

For the past two or three years, Karunya was moving about with serious and silent attitude. Sarada is surprised by his cheerful invitation and curious enough to go and see what is happening. So, she went to the place her son mentioned along with her husband.

Standing at the entrance of how valuable time and life are a Social Welfare Residential College, Karunya took his parents in. His friends, their parents, and many of the students were talking enthusiastically in the festive atmosphere that prevailed there.

The meeting started shortly after the arrival of the District Social Welfare Officer and the District Joint Collector. The chief guests lauded the teaching and direction of Karunya and his friends as a result of which fifteen students could secure a seat in Merit in the entrance test and got admission in reputed engineering colleges.

District Joint Collector said that the programs undertaken by his friends under the name 'Asara' are ideal and appreciable. The District Social Welfare Officer complimented the services of the participants of ASARA, criticizing some of the existing youth trends.

Karunya was congratulated for getting a job in a good company in Campus Selections for focusing on education along with inherent intelligence. Guests encouraged the Students to take Karunya and his group as an example, as an ideal and rise to the top in life.

Parents were invited on to the stage for felicitating them for giving birth to such pearl-like children who are devoting themselves to the purposeful tasks and congratulated them with bouquets.

Sarada didn't even dream this to happen. She is moved with excitement, she is overwhelmed with the touch of smiling Karunya . Ganga, the holy Ganges river is dancing with ecstasy between her eyelids.

CHAPTER SIX

The Burning Furnace

Janaki woke up with a startle. The pathetic cry of Sharwari in the dream moved like a whirlwind in her ears. Pressing her cheeks with both palms, she tried to suppress the turmoil in her heart. She cast a vexed look at her husband, snoring on the bed next to her.

She tried to sleep again, but all her efforts were in vain. The commotion in her mind is not allowing her to sleep. When she thought of her life, she felt as if she had been pushed to hell, she felt as if the ground under her feet was slipping away....

Yes! "They were pulling the ground under my feet by force", thought Janaki. Though the forces that were creating turmoil and shattering their lives which are entwined with the land were not known clearly, Janaki experienced the tumults caused by them every minute and trembled... Watching the innocent nature sleeping behind the veil of moonlight, she slithered into pondering.

Elders settled Janaki's marriage smashing her dreams of a college education. They thought that with fields, cattle, and a big old patterned residential building and with no dearth of basic amenities, she would have a comfortable life in the family she will be entering after marriage.

They felt that higher education was not possible for her. She could study so far because there was a high school in their village. If she was to be sent to town for higher education, people would start staring at their family with critical looks.

Fortunately, the bridegroom is from their place and she will live right in front of their eyes. With this view, they got her married to Srinivas.

Though she had a whim of marrying an employee, Janaki obeyed the elders and adjusted in her in-laws' home without a word of resistance. Her in-laws too, including their two daughters, never bothered her either for dowry or for any presents, never insulted her for anything, and never looked down upon her parents.

So, she also developed a kind of affection and respect for them. But even after having two children, what Janaki couldn't understand, was the mentality and attitude of Srinivas. He never expressed his love for her and never talked to her affectionately.

Srinivas, who never troubled her with his words or deeds, was an ideal man and an ideal husband in the eyes of others. But, Janaki too justified the role of an ideal wife efficiently and successfully never letting others realize that her ideal husband never treated her as a human being, never valued her thoughts and she never had a chance to talk regarding the decisions about her, her children and the family.

When he shifted the family to Kakinada, a nearby town from the village, without consulting her even once, with a pretext of children's education, he made her realize her limits. She could recognize unmistakably the role and place of a wife and a woman in that best man's opinion.

THE WAR

Though he never had any vices, Janaki thought that his obsession to live a grand life beyond their financial status was a sure vice.

He did not pay any heed to her warning that his vanity would destroy the family financially.

When two acres of land had to be sold for his undisciplined expenditure, his mother and father could not stand that. They pestered them to come back to the village from the city.

After retreating to the village as the circumstances never allowed him to deny the elders, they joined their daughter Sharwari and son in a hostel. Though Janaki couldn't bear the separation of her children, she consoled herself and felt peaceful about Srinivas, as they remained with his parents who could control him a bit.

But that peace never remained for a longer time. With a difference of a few months, one after the other, both his mother and father left the world. Janaki was in deep grief.

Despair, loneliness, and boundless fear about the future shook her completely. But, she didn't reveal it, appeared brave and strong. Though the weight of insult of not caring for her thoughts and opinion from the day of her marriage oozed out from the layers of her mind on and off, she suppressed it.

When she had put the lock deliberately to her mind, soul, and mouth, the lock handed over by her husband's sternness, no consequences in life shook her so easily.

But that too never went on for too long. She couldn't fulfil her wish regarding Sharwari's education. She thought of joining her in engineering college.

"No, a degree is enough to get her married to someone" when Srinivas said this, she could not open her mouth as she had lost the courage to argue long back. But when he fixed a rich match for Sharwari, forgetting his financial level and when he was ready to give ten acres out of eighteen acres of land they were possessing, as a dowry for a software engineer son-in-law, she dared to speak up.

"Let us find out a suitable match as per our status. If we give most of the property as dowry, what about the studies of our son?" Said Janaki. Srinivas looked at her with a relentless stare and he left the place without replying.

"My son is not bothered about the dowry, but he demands that the marriage should be performed in a very grand style.

So, make the arrangements carefully" when the bridegroom's parents warned Srinivas after they settled the marriage, Janaki was shocked. She knew what they meant by grand style and how expensive that could be

For three consecutive years, they had suffered losses due to natural calamities. Loans could not be repaid and the situation drifted from bad to worse

Is it an easy task to arrange the marriage with grandeur?! Loans in hundreds of thousands! No doubt, the price of the fields increased. Srinivas might have thought that If they could sell one or two acres, they could pay off the loans and perform the wedding in grandeur

His father used to look after the fields as his life and considered them as precious as their daughter. He always felt that going for debts or to sell the fields was a shameful thing and was a blot on the fame of the family.

When Srinivas sold a bit of the land to pay off the loans some time back, he felt ashamed and agonized. She knew that.

But what about this man! He never feels a pinch of it. Without an iota of hesitation, he took loans to perform his daughter's marriage. Janaki could not stop anything except experience the torture within.

She forgot the anguish temporarily looking at her daughter and son-in-law who were looking good and happy as though they were made for each other. She was taken aback by the pattern in which her husband went on fulfilling the greedy whims of their son's in law's parents, without any worry and fear.

After sending Sharwari to her in-laws' home, they took breathed a sigh of relief and thought of paying off the debts by selling the land. But untoward incidents occurred which posed as hanging knives on their necks.

The platform was ready to acquire thousands of acres of land for the special economic zone and the fields of their village too were included in that. There was a floating rumour that apart from snatching away the fields, they may make the people vacate the villages too.

This created turmoil in the village. Losing the fields and livelihood is one dimension of the problem. Another horrific dimension is leaving the native place where they had spent their entire life and the people entwined with their lives.

It was too hard for the villagers even to have a thought of parting with the affections and kinships that provide them the strength to live and face the troubles and problems and move forth to the unknown place. The very idea of having to leave their native village made them lifeless and shiver.

Janaki was too frightened. How to survive in a new place among strangers! How to live when the security of life is lost! She felt as if the trees nurtured as their life, are falling uprooted, a scene of elegant flower beds burning and a scene of carcasses heaping together.... Janaki felt her heart throbbing.

People, who were allocated land in the special economic zone, are announcing that they are going to start industries in this area very soon and the local youth will get plenty of jobs. A pronouncement went on that the area will be developed in such a way that each and everyone experiences affluence.

But, people like Janaki, who think pragmatically, very well know that it is a blatant lie. As she expected, the promises made to start industries and provide a good number of jobs, never made a start. ....Everyone, whose lands were taken by force, was perplexed....

What is this development that mars the livelihoods of hundreds of thousands of people? For whose benefit is this development intended? Janaki had many questions in her mind.

She could not understand the real plot in the beginning, but subsequently, she could sense the truth. She could understand for whose benefit the supposed development will be done.

She was too irritated to witness the actions of the government that hitherto have been protecting should be protecting the lives of the poor. When poor people were thrown away from their fields and homes treacherously and forcefully, it was a rude shock to see the Government remaining as a silent spectator and helping the powerful people from behind.

Janaki could also recognize the malice of acquiring thousands of acres of land when hundreds of acres could suffice for the industries.

But, whom so ever the affected people contacted, went on talking about the laws that the people could not understand. Nobody told them how the things that were not in the laws were also forced on them. Even after running from pillar to post, they could not get even a suggestion to have a solution.

As the days went on, everything was chaos and confusion. Janaki's mind turned frigid and she felt that she is She felt a vacuum in her mind. Suddenly uncontrollable grief, the fear of a demon attacking and grabbing everything in their possession, crept in.

Janaki recollected how one corporate company from western India acquired hundreds of acres of land near Kakinada a few years back and lured the people, telling the same stories about jobs and development. Later the company never started any industry.

All the lands acquired by them were used for the real estate business. If the land had been sold for the specified need, and if the promises were fulfilled, it is different. Now the value of the land that they had grabbed by force, turned into millions from thousands.

How pathetic it is to see the Democratic Government acting as a dirty broker, that lures, threatens, and somehow helps the greedy corporations to acquire the precious lands of the poor! When the grabbed land is not utilized as per the specified law, is it not the duty of the Government that is elected by the people, to guarantee justice to the people?

Is the democratic government working for the sake of a handful of rich people or the protection of the rights of a majority of Common people? ....Heat cropped up in Janaki's heart. History is repeating....she thought.

Till she received a phone call from her daughter Sarwari, Janaki could not figure out the Gravity of the situation. As it was an agreement to give ten acres of wetland to her daughter as dowry, if the government takes the land, her in-laws declared that she should be given a land of ten acres somewhere else.

When Sharwari expressed her in-laws' intention, Janaki thought that she was stuck in the middle of a storm. Not even a rupee of the debt taken for her marriage was paid back, the value of the fields that were outside the special economic zone spiked a lot. How could they buy ten acres of fertile land outside SEZ (special economic zone) with the peanut compensation received from the government

After knowing some of the facts, few farmers revolted denying the money offered as compensation and refused to sell their lands, some others who were lured and had already received compensation, demanded their lands to be returned.

Now they were well aware of the experiences of the local people in other special economic zones in the country. many meetings organized by social activists opened their eyes to their disastrous situation. In one of those meetings, Medha Patkar, well known across the country, addressed and made them clear about the real facts of special economic zones.

They knew that local unskilled people rarely got any jobs with a pretext that they lacked any skill or training. Even if one got any job, it would be low paid and industrialists were not bothered to provide skills training to them so that they would be eligible to secure high paid jobs, though they have to oblige to impart training to the local youth.

After having this realization, they bluntly refused the development that destroyed their lives. They went on fighting against the corporate forces which are strongly supported by the Government.

The affected people who were resisting by nonviolent means were arrested and sent to jail. Though they were subjected to innumerable hardships, they hooked on to their stand with courage.

They might succeed in their struggle, but what about the lives that shatter meanwhile? What about people like Janaki's family members, who remained in the middle of heaven and hell, who could neither cry openly nor come out of their secure homes and fight patiently or struggle to solve their problems?.......Pitch black darkness appeared in Janaki's eyes and an ocean of grief in her heart!

Though Sarwari never revealed openly, the mere thought of the dire consequences that might arise if the land was not given as promised churned Janaki's thoughts. She was completely engulfed by it.

The fear that if they failed to give the land as per the agreement, they may send her daughter back to the maternal home, instructing her to come back only when the land is given, started consuming all her energies.

How to save her daughter's family life? How can her son survive in this materialistic world without fields and proper education? How

Can she and her husband survive for the rest of their lives? Answerless questions bothered Janaki.

If the common people can't get some space in this modern progressive world that boasts of the so-called development and if the less powerful and marginalized sections of people don't have an alternative except to die, what is the meaning of this development?

If you need to get tensed up with the panic of facing havoc any moment, or with the fear of snatching your life earnings or properties by unscrupulous people, why allow that development in the first instance?

When the ray of hope of security to the future life is blurred in an atmosphere perpetuated by some of the neo rich cruel people, is there any alternative except to vehemently reject that development? Shouldn't we have a world where all the people can live without fear?

How can common people, who have lost all their strength, escape from the clutches of the strong forces that are creating, supporting, and maintaining this sort of world? How can they fight against them? How can the common people encounter strong corrupt forces of this nature?

Will the hapless common people catching their hungry bellies with their thin hands, remain forever in this manner? Will the hunger kindle anger? Will the frail hands that hold the empty bellies transform into a strong fist wrapped with a layer of revenge? Won't the blazing hearts explode? Janaki's heart was like a furnace.

CHAPTER SEVEN

Fragrance

The fragrance of incense and the fragrance of jasmine petals, accompanied by a gentle breeze from the pool, were pervading the Shiva temple. Silence replaced the rhythmic sounds of chanting hymns and praising of Lord Shiva. The dim light of pyramids, an earthenware saucer containing oil and a wick, used as a lamp, on the doorstep of the temple, is dimming.

Rajeshwari, who was lying on her side with her elbow under her head, was crying as she blocked her mouth with the loose end of her sari. Slowly her cry changed to sobs with mild sound and her flanks were moving up and down

Gauri, who was sleeping, keeping her hand on her mother's waist, woke up. She looked around anxiously to observe whether anyone sleeping a little further away was disturbed by the sound of her mother's sobs and had not woken up. She was relaxed when she noticed that they were fast asleep. Moving aside her mother, she turned her mother's face towards her and wiped her tears.

"Don't cry, mother! Calm your heart, go to sleep."Gouri's mother, Rajeshwari restrained herself with the touch of her comforting daughter, gently moving her palm over her back. She slowly fell asleep trying to get out of the grief. But Gauri couldn't sleep due to running waves of thoughts lingering in her mind

Rajeshwari, who married Raghuramaiah at the age of fifteen, was very cordial and obedient to her in-laws and friendly with her husband's sisters and younger brothers. They reciprocated her with the same love and affection.

Rajeshwari and Raghuramaiah shared the joys and sorrows of their relatives and neighbours and helped them to the best of their capacity. They received the same reciprocation from them.

Apart from doing household chores, Rajeswari went to the farm whenever there was work and actively participated in planting, weeding, cutting the crop etc.

The couple was blessed with four sons before Gouri was born... Raghuramaiah and Rajeswari were happy and proud of having four sons like Dasaradha Maharaj, father of Lord Sriram.

The prevailing ideology in the society was if one had more children, that too, male children, more earnings. They hoped that their sons would be engaged in cultivation along with them and they would prosper better than others in the village. That is why they did not pay much attention to the education of their sons.

Gauri, as a child, was like a jumping doll, roaming freely among the fields, trees and flowering plants, laughing, giggling and chatting with friends. Gouri joined in the school and was studying with keen interest.

She came to know that her Telugu teacher, who joined in the school recently, would love to teach music, Gauri approached her with a request to become her student and started to learn music with a passion.

After attaining menarche, Gauri, an eighth-grader, was not allowed to go to the co-education school and was asked to learn cooking and other household work from her mother and aunts.

Gauri though felt sad for some time for her inability to continue studies, compromised with the tradition of the community and pursued learning of music. She was very active and pretty with her youthful looks and had learned to tidy up everything.

Bhaskaran, the son of Venkataramaiah, from a neighbouring village, had seen Gauri in a marriage function of a relative and told his parents that he liked Gouri and would marry her.

Raghuramaiah felt happy about the alliance. When one of the Bhaskaram's relatives approached, he readily agreed... As the boy's family had a life without any deprivation, lands, big house and a good reputation in the village, Gouri's parents had no hesitation to get their daughter married to Bhaskaran.

They also felt happy for their only daughter living closer to them. Marriage was performed following the traditions and according to their financial status. Gouri went to her husband's house with plenty of dreams and hopes.

* * *

After Gouri left along with her husband the house seemed empty to her parents. They were missing her a lot as she was always around them, expressing joy for every small positive thing and singing with ecstasy while doing something or other with ease and aesthetics.

Raghuramaiah was trying to focus on increasing the family income by involving his sons in the cultivation. He had taken another fifteen acres of land for lease adding to their land for cultivation. His elder two sons were enthusiastic to support their father's wish.

They were toiling in all the activities, from ploughing to weeding and harvesting. Raghuramaiah didn't compromise in investing at any stage, whether it is for fertilizers, pesticides or wages to the farmworkers. But, just before harvesting produce, a sudden storm swept away and ruined the whole crop.

The family was utterly disappointed with the end result. They couldn't repay even a minute part of the debt taken for investment. Moreover, they were deprived of enough produce for their sustenance and keeping the livestock alive. The two elder sons, who had been working tirelessly along with their father and mother, were drowned in depression.

In the second year, there was moderate yield, but the selling price was less, in the next year the crop was destroyed by locusts, and in the fourth year the crop didn't yield much, Raghuramaiah collapsed with the burden of debts, but the hope in him didn't die completely.

The two elder sons concluded with the experience in the previous four successive years, that they would not sustain in the village. They had decided to migrate to the city and make their livelihood do some work or other.

They got placing as watchmen in the apartment complexes. The third son also lost confidence in having a living in the village and migrated to the city after two years and joined in a mechanic shop as an apprentice. The fourth son completed his training at ITI as a fitter and got a temporary job with meagre wages in a factory.

After some time, Gouri's life, which she aspired to be like a melodious song, transformed into a song of injuries, filled with pain and despair. Her voice was dumbfounded by the ridicule and shouting by her husband.

Bhaskaram's started drifting away from Gauri after the birth of two daughters in a row and had extramarital relations with other women. He was drunk most of the time and was wandering in the village and nearby town aimlessly, without doing any work.

Sometimes he abused Gouri with bad words and hit her on and off. His father, who could control him a little bit, died some time back. When his mother tried to tell him to behave properly, he wouldn't hesitate even to confront her with abusive language.

Of late, a new vice is added to the existing vices. Bhaskaram was engaged in moving with the local leaders of a political party and spending the money in a wasteful manner. As a result, there was a conflict between the brothers and they partitioned the property and started to live separately.

Now Bhaskaram was showing all his frustrations by abusing Gowri. After some time, the situation had reached a point when Gauri was unable to bear his aggression anymore.

Rajeshwari was heartbroken by her daughter came back to their house. When everyone preached her daughter that she should stay at her husband's place as an ideal wife, however much suffering she had to experience and do her duty to try to correct her husband with patience and love. They declared that it would be against her honour to run away to her mother's place.

Gouri showed her visible injuries to her mother, leaving aside the invisible injuries to her heart and mind, "I can't stand it anymore mother! If I try to be patient and endure, even if he talks nonsense after fully drunk, he would scold me and children with horrible words, if I retort, he would be much more aggressive and attacked me.

He would snatch away whatever I earn from doing work in the fields to feed my children. How much and how many years to endure like this! For how many days I can starve my children? How can I be alive without eating for days together?" Gauri cried pitiably.

Rajeswari remained silent for the fear of her sons and their wives and the people outside. No matter how much she desired to hide her daughter under her wings, she couldn't protect her even after pleading with her husband.

When Gauri was pushed back to her husband's home, she was like a goat walking to be sacrificed. But, she had returned with a broken mind and injured body within six months. This time Raghuramaiah also was plumbed in deep grief. He spent sleepless nights thinking about the future of his daughter and her children

"Mother! Please take care of my children for at least one year. Maithili Madam, daughter of Mr. Kanakarajui promised to show me work at Hyderabad. I would not be a burden for you for long. Will you do this favour to me mother?" Gouri asked.

Rajeshwari cried keeping her arms around her daughter "God, Why my daughter's life is so pathetic?" She was tormented by the fear that if Gauri is forced to go back to her drunkard husband, she might take an extreme step about her life and might even commit suicide leaving her children as orphans.

The hope that there would be a change in her son-in-law and that he would take care of his wife and children vanished long back. He didn't stop his vices of addiction to alcohol and playing cards. His weakness for women became notorious.

Rajeshwari was quite aware of their dwindling financial position and their inability to take care of them for long. Hence, agreed to her daughter's proposal reluctantly, despite the fears about their daughter having the threat of facing character assassination when she steps into the outside world. Raghuramayya agreed to his daughter's decision with a heavy heart.

However, Gauri's brothers did not readily agree. 'Why to ruin family life and come out? How about our honour if she works as the housemaid in unknown houses with male members?' They questioned.

"Did I leave my husband without any reason? Doing bad things, going along wrong paths and being addicted to vices is against honour. To live with the earnings of hard work would never be against honour. I do not have education, assets and people who would support for the sustenance of me and my children.

As there was no other option, I chose this path. I have faith in the strength of my hands. I am confident that I can live with my hard work and give a reasonably good life for my children." Gauri Said angrily.

Gauri knows that her elder brother's wife Sumathi and second brother's wife Ramya were working in the apartments where their husbands were working as watchmen and their families were running without any deficit due to that. Gauri did not understand why it was against honour if she worked in others' houses when it wasn't against honour when her sisters-in-law work in the same way.

'Are my brothers giving judgment that I should be prostrated at my husband's feet even if he beats or kills me? ... Without being a burden on anybody, I want to lead my life depending on my hard work.' Gouri said to herself. When her husband came to know that Gauri had decided to move away from home and live independently, he made a big hue and cry and demanded her to return home.

He threatened her to kill if he didn't return home. Gauri remained silent no matter how much he yelled. Her silence provoked him even more. After seeing his indecent behaviour, her decision turned out to be stronger.

* * *

Gauri went to Hyderabad with Mythili, who gave her shelter in her house. After coming to know about Gouri's clean and tidy work and skilful cooking, few other housewives in the adjacent flats offered her work.

Gauri was working nonstop from early in the morning till it was dark. Gauri used to do every work for Mythili with great gratitude. Mythili was very much impressed by her courage and dedication to stay unmoved by the problems surrounding her.

After knowing the lives of other women working in the apartments, Gouri realized that the essence of lives of most of the women working there was almost the same though with different grades.

Gauri's perseverance increased when she learned that all these women had migrated to the city due to their husband's addictions and violence in addition to the decreasing chances of livelihood in their villages and were struggling to keep their children alive and come up in life.

After earning some money, Gauri rented a room near the apartment complex on Maithili's advice and brought the children to enrol them in a nearby Government school... Gauri's sole focus is on the golden future of her children, just as Arjuna's focus was on the eye of the bird before throwing the arrow.

Despite the hard work all along with his life, Raghuramaiah could not earn enough to ask his daughter from the city and support her family. When he came to know that his son-in-law and people in the village are spreading rumours about his daughter's character, he felt distressed.

He warned his wife not to reveal these rumours to his daughter when she comes to the village. But somehow they reached Gouri's ears. Though temporarily got agitated, she became more assertive. Gauri never went home unless it was very necessary.

Even when Gauri went there, as she already learned the skill to live facing the adversaries and regardless of what others comment about her, either directly or indirectly.

Her elder brothers living in different parts of the same city never bothered to call their only sister and enquired about her well being. They didn't invite her to their homes to stay with them for one or two days and present her a sari, as per the custom if not with love.

Some times Gouri used to feel bad thinking about her brothers, with tears rolling on her cheeks. But immediately she hurriedly wiped the tears with a sentimental feeling that her tears would harm her brother' families

Though she was hurt by their behaviour, for her, everything else seemed unimportant and too trivial before her firm determination to stand erect facing the tidal waves of hardships and to sustain the zest for life.

Gauri, who skillfully escapes from those who try to subdue her taking advantage of her loneliness, had anxiety about her two young daughters. Despite the lack of proper food, nice clothes and jewellery, they were looking pretty and attracted people by the brilliance of their early youth, electrifying attitude.

Gouri was worried about their safety; she was frightened with the thoughts that her daughters might get trapped in unnecessary and dangerous situations and relations that mar their future. She was aware of the incidents of girls being misled and deceived, harassed in the name of love and even sexually assaulted and killed brutally in the present-day society.

Gouri wanted to educate them about the importance of education by telling that they shouldn't neglect their studies for the sake of temporary lures and get distracted and that they should remember that education is the most powerful tool to ascend the ladder of success in life.

But again, she remained silent in despair, thinking that she didn't have enough education and worldly knowledge to guide them properly. In a moment she picks up her confidence and realizes that the real-life experience is the most eligible aspect to show them the right path.

Gouri's elder daughter, Renuka understands her goal and studies diligently and also supports the family by earning some money by giving tuitions to the younger children during her out of college hours.

But her second daughter, Meena was obsessed with decorating herself to look beautiful like movie heroines. The attraction of her second daughter for an expensive life was not palatable to Gauri.

'It would be the most tragic incident of my life if Meena would slip walking on the rocks of the glittering world. I am desperately fighting with all odds of my life for the sake of these children. It would be disastrous if they fail me' Gouri was trying to cope up with her disturbing thoughts.

* * *

Raghuramaiah died of a sudden heart attack. When the news of her father's death was intimated, Gouri went to the village along with her daughters to have a last glimpse of her loving father. Gauri sat at her father's feet and cried incessantly.

She recollected her childhood and the happiest days she had spent with him along with her mother and brothers. She felt that she lost all her energy by her father's demise, remembering how he loved all his children with special affection towards his only daughter.

She remembered the gentle touch of her father comforting her when she was adamant to get anything. She felt that she lost the only support she had so far. She felt that she was orphaned.

She recollected the death of her husband two years ago when she sat near his corpse with detachment. She was like a stone, not having any emotions.

Gauri slowly got up, went to her mother, hugged and tried to comfort her mother. Rajeswari was looking stunned after the sudden loss of her husband with whom she had been living for almost fifty years. Tears welled up in Gouri's eyes.

When the father's cremation was over, all the brothers went away, elder two telling that they had to get back to the city as the president and secretary of the apartment complexes where they were working, asked them to come back soon.

The third and fourth brothers went away with some flimsy pretext. All of them told their mother that they would be back for the tenth-day ceremony. Rajeswari asked her daughters-in-law not to go, as the villagers and relatives find fault with their behaviour if they wouldn't be there till 10th-day ceremony. But they left silently without telling her

Gouri was wavering whether to go for the sake of the two old couples in two flats, who were dependent on her or to stay with her mother in this tragic phase. After her brothers' families left leaving their mother all alone, she decided to stay back.

She didn't want her mother to be insulted. She sent her daughters to the city telling them to serve the old people in the flats and attend the college.

***

Despite not being able to earn enough money for their sustenance, Raghuramaiah was respected for his hard work, integrity and honesty by all the relatives and villagers. Gouri wanted his last rights and rituals to be performed as per the tradition of their community with the involvement of all near and dear to Raghuramaiah.

Her mother felt happy on hearing Gouri's proposal. She called her brothers and said the same thing. They replied as if they were not that interested in those rituals and said that it would be a waste of money. Gauri found their negative attitude towards the rituals, her father strongly believed.

Then the issue was how to raise money for the expenditure of the ceremony. Her brothers sold all the land they possess 1 year back, as there was no proper income on agriculture and as their parents were not able to work in the fields.

They shared the amount, keeping one hundred thousand rupees aside for the parents. Her parents wanted to give a small share of the amount to their daughter who was living without any support from any corner. But their sons vehemently rejected their proposal.

Gouri was concerned about the money after estimating the cost for the rituals and food for the people who would attend the ceremony. She didn't know whether her parents had any money with them. She was hesitant to ask her mother.

But as there was no other alternative, she handed over the paper with the estimate to her mother. Rajeswari gave her the amount left with her and asked Gouri to make necessary arrangements.

Gauri's brothers came on the day before the ceremony. They were annoyed about looking at the arrangements made spending the money without their involvement but remained silent.

No one from Rajeswari's maternal home was in a position to attend the ceremony except her brother's son Venu. After the ceremony was over, as per the custom, Rajeshwari's parents or brothers should take her to their home, keep her for a couple of days and present her a sari.

As her parents died and her brother was unable to travel, his son, Venu attended the ceremony. But Venu hurriedly went off though one of their relatives reminded him to take Rajeswari along with him.

Gouri's brothers wanted to put the house, where their parents were living, for sale. On the next day after the ceremony, they were getting ready to go back, but there was no word of taking their mother along with them.

Gouri was shocked to see the indifference exhibited by her brothers towards their mother. She also needed to go for her work immediately as she couldn't lose her work, staying in the village any further. But she was hesitant, as she was skeptical about her brothers' attitude. If they wouldn't take the mother along with them where would she live? If the house is sold, where would she get shelter?

Gouri didn't want to think negatively about her brothers and hoped that they would take her with them. Then she packed her things and went to the bus stand to catch the bus early and reach home before the sunset.

While waiting for the bus, she was worried about the possibility of her brothers not taking their mother with them. She was frightened with the sight of her helpless mother collapsing in despair.

'How would she survive without anyone around and without enough money to sustain?' Gouri couldn't bear that. She didn't want to leave her mother in the village and go mercilessly. She wanted to take mother to her home if she was left alone by her sons.

Gouri was wondering whether her mother would accept her proposal. Her bereaved mother along with her father used to say proudly that they had four sons like the Dasaradh Maharaj.

Gouri Knows the ingrained feeling of the community that the parents should live with their sons who inherit the family name and property, and it is disgraceful to live in the house of daughters. Hesitant for a while, Gouri took an instant decision and returned back to her mother.

Her brothers' family members, who were going to the bus stand by Auto rickshaws, avoided looking at her directly

On her way, she stopped at the temple, met the priest, narrated the condition and asked him to tell a way out to avoid criticism from the relatives. He told her that if her mother sleeps in the Shiva temple for one night, she can be taken to any one's house, not necessarily to her sons' house.

Then, with a sigh of relief, Gouri took her mother to Shiva temple to sleep there. Gouri's thoughts were disrupted as she saw her mother waking up

"Mother! Don't cry. Be happy with me and my children. Don't feel bad to live with your daughter. I promise that I will take care of you as long as I live. Mother! You are my third daughter" Told Gouri with a loving smile. Rajeswari nodded her head approvingly, keeping her arms around Gouri's shoulders and looking at her with moist eyes.

* * *

The fragrant Parijatham flowers falling on the ground in the temple garden and the musical chirping of the sparrows comforted Gouri and her mother. Just then the darkness of the night was getting dispelled by the rays of positive vibrations. The doors of Shiva temple were opened.

* * *

About The Author

Dr Vijayalakshmi Aluriis an Ob./Gy. Specialist, practising in private set up for fifty years. She served thousands of women belonging to three generations and as a friend, philosopher and guide to these women have the fortune of fond bond with them.

As such she has the most valuable opportunity of first-hand information of the lives of women with their struggles, pains and vulnerabilities and also the successes of strong and emancipated women.

As an avid reader of literature, she developed a passion to write and had been writing for 58 years. Her personal and professional life had been profoundly influenced by literature to transform to be more humane.

She strongly believes that the literature has the power of influencing the people positively or negatively, hence, she affirms that the author should write anything with social responsibility and should ascertan before writing whether her/his piece of work is promoting the good or the bad in the society.

She also believes that the Literature should be the voice of the voiceless people. She assumes that good Literature purifies the soul and environs of the people to make this world a better place.

Dr **Vijayalakshmi Aluri**is a writer of around **150short stories, 4novels, 4health education books**

'Matrutvam'(Advices to the Pregnant women**), The story of our body, 'Adolescent girls' health'- inregional language** and **Adolescents' Health and Behavior** in **English**and **translator**of **world-famous health education books**from English to Telugu,(**'Where there is no doctor'**,

ABOUT THE AUTHOR

'Where women have no doctor', and 'Where there is no Psychiatrist') published by **Hyderabad Book Trust** and (**The story of blood, Thumpa and sparrow and Tortoise wins again**) published by **National Book Trust of India.**

1,00,000 copies of 'Adolescent girls' health' were distributed to the **high school, college and out of school girls** with the financial assistance extended by the **Govt. and non Govt. organizations**

Her very first story (**Malupu-Twist**) won a prize in Diwali short story competition conducted by a popular Telugu weekly, Andhra Prabha

Many of her stories and talks were broadcasted by **A.I.R., Visakhapatnam** and **Vijayawada.**

Had the opportunity of participating in **Kavisammelanams** twice, organized by **Doordarshan, Hyderabad**.

Wrote a column for many years in **Vanitha,** a magazine for women, by **Chandamama group of publications**, with the title **Arogya Vijayalu.**

Participated in many TV discussions related to women's issues, health and literature

Mrs Sujatha, M.phil student of Telugu Dept., Nagarjuna University, selected **Dr. Aluri Vijayalakshmi's literature as** her **Thesis subject** and got her degree.

Essays titled "**The impact of cinema on society**" first **published by A.P. State Sahitya Academy,** was later included in the **text book of P.U.C., Banglore university** and another essay, titled "**If a doctor is also a writer**", first published in the **souvenir of Raja lakshmi foundation, Madras,** was included in the **text book of B.A., Open University, Hyderabad.**

Name of **Dr.Vijayalakshmi Aluri** is included in "**Who is who of Indian writers**" and "**who is who of Indian

Translators" published by **Kendra Sahitya Academy** of Indian Government.

She was **Winner of World Bank's Innovative projects competition,** the title of the project being "**Adolescent girls as promoters of basics in feminine hygiene, health and nutrition**", one of the **20 winners** among **1500** submitted projects and was **adjudged as "one of the 5 best implemented projects"** by the World Bank and was projected as a **model project** in all the countries where world Bank's activities make their presence.